HELL BENT FOR DEMONS

THE DEVIL'S DAUGHTER (BOOK 2)

G.A. CHASE

BAYOU MOON PRESS, LLC

Copyright © 2018 by G.A. Chase

First Edition 2018

Cover Art by Ravven

Editing by Red Adept

ISBN eBook: 978-940299-70-9

ISBN print: 978-1-940299-69-3

This book is a work of fiction. Names, characters, places, and incidents are products of the author's imagination or are used fictitiously. Any resemblance to actual events, locals, business establishments, or persons, living or dead, are entirely coincidental.

Bayou Moon Press, LLC

ABOUT THIS BOOK

After ridding the swamp of a serial-killing demon, badass Sere Mal-Laurette has moved to New Orleans to put some distance between the interdimensional beacon of her soul and the hellmouth. Hell, however, has other plans for her when a new horde of beasts is unleashed.

Sere will have to knock the rust off her fighting skills if she hopes to save herself and humanity from a fate worse than death. But she soon learns she can't do it alone, and she's going to need more than the help of a bartending former Navy SEAL who makes her weak in the knees. The bikers and gator hunters she's been using for sport during her bar brawls are going to take some serious convincing to join her cause—even if they are the ones most at risk.

By relying on those closest to her to repair her doppelgänger body, hunt down the demons that are out to get her, and protect her soul from the loas of the dead, Sere just might learn something about what it means to be human.

Sere Mal-Laurette's heart beat in time to the music from the club below. The nightly jazz-rock fusion wafted through the bargeboard floor of her loft above the Scratchy Dog nightclub like a voodoo spell calling her forth. She pushed open the perpetually stuck French doors of the dormer roof and stepped out onto the one-person balcony for her evening vigil. Energy from the crowd below infused the warm late-summer humidity and had her swaying to the rhythm of the street. She closed her eyes and breathed in the rich aromas of alcohol and gumbo from the street vendors. Every aspect of life on Frenchmen Street had proved intoxicating, and the experience had dulled her abilities. And she didn't even care. At least being in the city made her less of a beacon for the demons trying to find their way out of hell.

But her nightly foray to the balcony wasn't about being filled with human energy. As she opened her eyes and stared out over the French Quarter rooftops, a chill struck so deeply into her chest that she thought her heart had frozen. "Fucking assgängers!" The green sparks on the horizon looked like a Saint Patrick's Day fireworks display. Unfortunately, that drunken free-for-all had happened months before. After witnessing twelve weeks and three days of sunsets, she had begun to hope she was free of hell's denizens.

She gripped the wrought-iron railing to focus her frustration and stared intently out toward the swamp far beyond the city. *Seven explosions. The same number as the people Monty murdered. That can't be a coincidence.*

"Come on down and dance for us! Show us your moves." As with every night, the longer she stood on the third-floor balcony, the more rambunctious the suitors of both sexes became. The fact that she usually gave in to their nightly temptations had only emboldened the youthful partiers.

"Not tonight. I've got work to do." She returned to the loft and changed out of the party clothes and into her leather motorcycle-riding pants, halter top, and gatorskin boots complete with a combat knife sheathed inside. The rest of her gear lay in the middle of the saggy seldom-used mattress. Her belongings didn't amount to much: a set of motorcycle saddlebags with two changes of clothing inside, a four-barrel sawed-off shotgun and leather holster that she secured around her thigh, a matching bullet belt that hung low across her hips, and finally, a bedroll with a pump-action blaster protruding out the end. She left the backpack filled with excess shotgun shells on the bed. Her fighting instructor, Joe Cazenave, had taught her long ago never to put all of her ammunition in one hidden stash. She had caches of supplies along the swamp route in case she ran low.

"Time to go." Sere had to stretch all the way to her tiptoes to put her hand over the loft's rough-hewn wooden beam. A two-foot-long canebrake rattlesnake slithered across her wrist and down her forearm. He didn't stop until he'd undulated across her neck and into the saddlebag slung around her shoulder. "Come on. I don't have time for your laziness. I know it's nearly nightfall, but you can't use your cold-blooded lethargy as an excuse in this heat." The second snake flicked her hand with his tongue. "I swear, I'm going to leave without you if you don't get that rattle shaking."

The snake made an overly dramatic fall from the rafter and along her arm but caught himself before crashing into her head. He coiled his body onto her shoulder and flicked her ear with his tongue as his sign of affection.

"You'll be happier once we're back out in the swamp. Now, hop to, mister. We've got demons to chase."

Sere took one last look around the room. She'd only agreed to occupy the human-sized Victorian birdcage as a way of getting Aunt Kendell off her back. She shook her head as the memory of their conversation played out.

"I'll be more at ease knowing you've got a safe place to crash." Kendell had struggled to get the old skeleton key to line up with the lock's tumblers.

Climbing the two flights of dimly lit, creaky stairs would have proven enough of a security feature, but Sere watched dutifully as Kendell finally managed to get the misaligned loft door open. The overly caring woman honestly believed safety was possible for Sere, and Sere had bought into the delusion.

"I can take care of myself." Sere fondled the butt of the knife stashed in her boot. The reflex probably wasn't the best way for her to calm Kendell's fears, but she found it hard to control.

"I'm not talking about idiots like Thomas. His abduction of you was moronic."

Sere was still itching for a rematch with Professor Yates's doppelgänger assistant, even if he was nothing more than a phantom possessing the real person. "Then why did you come barreling in to rescue me?" she asked.

"We couldn't let you kill him. Some lines shouldn't be crossed."

"Fair enough, but if you're not worried about humans attacking me, why bother with this dusty cage?"

Like a magician performing her act, Kendell had pulled the yellowed bedsheet off the French doors. Light had flooded into the dreary apartment. "Because this building belongs to me and Myles. This may be the only room in all of New Orleans where the loas of the dead dare not enter. You can sleep here."

Sleep. That's a good one, Sere thought. But the promise of keeping the dreaded lords of the dead off her ass was enough incentive to keep her in the big city. She hadn't anticipated becoming addicted to the human energy that constantly surrounded her as well.

Before entering the small bathroom, she bolted the front door from the inside. Though there was no need for covert behavior, finding alternate ways in and out of the loft helped keep her focused. Dangers—both human and supernatural—would be lurking from every shadow in the dimly lit French Quarter.

She opened the frosted glass window above the toilet, pushed her saddlebags and bedroll through, and climbed over the porcelain commode. Squeezing past the chipped paint and rotting wood frame sent adrenaline pumping into her blood. Outside the small window, she secured her belongings over her shoulders. The roof angled sharply down toward the courtyard behind the club. She knew every handhold and loose piece of mortar in the brick walls. Hell's version of the walled-in open space had been where she'd endured Joe's combat training when she was just a child.

Too obvious an escape route. Skipping the courtyard, she scurried along the rusted gutter to the side of the club. Without breaking stride, she jumped over the five-foot alleyway between buildings. Her mercenary training had become so ingrained that she didn't always know when her memory was pulling up Joe's teachings and when it was her interpretation. *Stealth isn't just about being unobserved. When noise is unavoidable, imitate nature. People will happily discount the sounds of a rat outside their window rather than accept the need to investigate a burglar.*

The lesson, however, hadn't taken into account that at 109 pounds plus belongings, Sere couldn't put as much trust in the hundred-year-old structures as a two-pound rat could. Her alligator boot went straight through a piece of Swiss-cheesed gutter, causing her to lose her balance. Even curling her body into a tumbling-gymnastic fall failed to prevent the snap of her arm as she landed on the concrete sidewalk. To avoid being seen, she continued her roll until she was under the wooden porch.

"Fuck." She held her wrist and slowly twisted it to confirm the break. "Nothing I can do for it now. Joe is going to kick my ass. Guess I shouldn't have skipped out on those last training sessions."

She double-checked her bags to make sure her snakes and gun were still okay before sneaking out of hiding like a raccoon starting her nightly prowl. If people had noticed her fall, they weren't rushing to her aid. *Not the ideal escape route, I guess, but at least I don't have to explain my night's plans to Aunt Kendell.* Sere kept to the shadows as she hurried along the street lined with colorfully painted old homes.

At the plywood-covered doorway of an abandoned cottage, she checked to make sure she hadn't been followed. The security light over the entrance, which she'd knocked out a week before, hadn't been changed. With a backward thrust of her good elbow against the frame, she popped open the makeshift door. Staring out from under the caved-in ceiling was the headlight of her Triton café racer.

She snuck in, tossed her saddlebags over the back seat, and bungeed her bedroll onto the front fender. "The team's back together." The cheesy line had become her rallying cry.

Wheeling the motorcycle out of its hiding spot, however, proved challenging with a busted arm. The snakes shook their rattles in displeasure at the lurching exit. "You're right. I'm not ready. Before I head out to the swamp to confront whatever just escaped hell, I need a refresher course with Joe. And I can't fight him until my arm's healed.

I guess we'll just have to hole up somewhere until morning."

~

THE SWAMP BECKONED like a warm bath, but finding rest among the rivers, cypress groves, and wild animals wouldn't quicken Sere's healing. If she was to face Joe—and after him hell's demons—she needed to be fully functional.

Fuck it. Instead of heading for the freeway and the peace of the bayou, she turned down Esplanade toward the river. *Maybe I'll get lucky and the professor won't be in. He can't possibly spend every moment in those dilapidated shipping offices.*

The approach to the seemingly deserted warehouse was lined with hidden detectors and more blatant video cameras designed specifically to identify Sere and her demon brethren. She pulled the motorcycle alongside the building, looked up into the round black dome, and smiled in case there was someone doing guard duty at the monitor.

Before heading in, she reached into her saddlebag and pulled out the lazy snake. "If there's no one home, I'll need you as my lookout." The serpent coiled around her neck like a scaly scarf.

With one quick thrust of her combat knife between the boarded-up glass door and metal frame, she gained access to the office. "Anyone here?" she called out.

All she got in response was the ticking of the professor's equipment as it projected data from the living world into hell's virtual reality. She headed to the medical cabinet at the back of the office. "I fucking hate this."

She popped the latch as she'd done with the front door. Inside the white-and-red locker were boxes of wire-laced cloth, computer cords, metal probes, and all manner of sensors designed to read Sere's vital functions. She felt a bit like Frankenstein's monster staring into the laboratory where he'd been created.

On the highest shelf were neatly stacked bundles of technology-infused ACE bandages. She grabbed the top one and headed for the professor's workbench. "I really fucking hate this."

The snake around her neck craned its body around so it could look her in the eye and hissed.

"Yes, I know I repeated myself. Deal with it." With only one working hand, she found wrapping the cloth around her broken arm a challenge. Even when she thought she had it right, she pulled loose the Velcro tab and rebandaged the arm. By the third wrapping, she gave up trying to do it perfectly. "It's not like anyone's around to judge my efforts."

She reached over to the archaic computer and booted up the hard drive. Of the roughly one million files representing every person in New Orleans, only Jennifer Ellen Cranston had her own tab at the bottom of the screen—right next to the one labeled Sere's Recovery.

Sere plugged the bandage into the USB port and opened the file regarding her personal projection. "I really, really fucking hate this a lot."

The snake slithered down her arm and onto the table as if indicating it had heard enough of her whining.

"You're right. I need to face my doppelgänger condition

like a warrior. No point in putting this off." She opened her personal tab and hit the file marked Connection to Real.

JENNIFER CRANSTON SWERVED her mom-mobile and hit the brakes to avoid slamming into the stopped cars on the Crescent City Connection incline. "Shoot. That was close. Are you okay, baby?"

"Mom! Stop calling me that." Bobby was just old enough to start being belligerent.

Thank God I never had kids in hell, Sere thought from behind Jennifer's eyes.

The woman's headshake reminded Sere that she was supposed to be the silent energy parasite. Anything she thought could too easily distract the airheaded, hair-dyed, post-popular girl.

"What a strange train of thought." Jennifer rubbed her forehead, feeling for a bump that she might have sustained from hitting it on the steering wheel.

Of course you didn't hit your head, you cock-loving, moronic ex-cheerleader.

Jennifer turned the sedan back in line with traffic and tentatively eased the accelerator down as if she wasn't sure she remembered how to drive. A beat-up truck shot into the gap in front of her.

My God, woman. You are an even worse driver than you are a cook. Sere desperately wanted to take the reins and stomp on the gas.

"Are you wearing your seat belt, my love?"

9

"Like you'd ever let me leave it off." Bobby's voice had a high-pitched arrogance that made Sere want to slap him across the face.

To Sere's surprise, Jennifer punched the gas and turned hard left to cut in front of a slow-moving semi. The big truck blew its air horn, but not before Jennifer had made another lane change into the carpool lane.

"Jesus, Mom. Are you trying to get us killed?"

Shut up, you little pip-squeak, Sere thought.

"Just trying to get home before your father. You know how he hates it when his dinner gets overcooked." From behind Jennifer's calm façade, Sere could tell the woman's singsong voice was her way of telling her son to politely fuck off.

Sere felt something yank hard backward against her gut like a parasail that had just been deployed, pulling her out of the boat that was Jennifer's thoughts. *Fucking connectus interruptus.*

"Why the hell did you do that?" she yelled. The friction burn on her skin from the bandage being ripped off hurt worse than the broken arm.

Professor Yates threw the strip of cloth clear across the room. "You're a damn fool! There's an order to these things, you know. Without the security programs being in place, your thoughts could seep into your real's. The hard line between where she leaves off and you begin needs to be maintained."

Sere rubbed her arm. It still hurt below the skin, but at least the bones felt like they'd knitted back together. "I had my snake in case something went wrong."

"How is he gonna know you've gotten lost in the connection? He's a snake, not a mind reader." The professor's wiry gray hair took on an even more electrified look as he shook his head. "Besides, the connection isn't just about you. If the safeguards aren't put in place first, your real could end up thinking she's losing her mind. People aren't used to random voices inside their heads." He brought up the Jennifer Ellen Cranston file. "Why do you think I keep her file readily at hand? I have to know if our actions are infecting her."

Sere looked at the readouts of the mundane life her real was leading. "What are you looking for?" No one knew Jennifer as thoroughly as Sere. Maybe she'd be able to spot something beyond the housewife's lifestyle.

"Anything that seems like it would have come from you. If she were to take up shooting, for example, or if she cut her hair short and let it return to its natural dark-red color."

Sere wondered if driving like a maniac counted. "You think she's going to abandon her family, move out to the swamp, and worry about seeing demons at every turn?" she asked.

"That would be an extreme example, but yes, that is exactly the scenario that worries me. What you see when you look at the doppelgängers could become her reality as well."

Sere closed her eyes in frustration. "I'll go easy on her."

The professor was right, as always. If Jennifer developed Sere's ability to see the doppelgängers with translucent skin, she'd probably check herself into a mental hospital.

"We need her to continue on with her life as usual. If she

gets put under a doctor's care, he could easily prescribe her antipsychotics. If she loses touch with reality, I might not be able to use her for your body's blueprint."

Sere looked at her healed arm. "What would that mean for me?"

Professor Yates turned to the bank of computers that filled the hallway. "The easiest and fastest method of fixing your boo-boos is to hook you up directly to her energy, but I've got enough data on her to take care of any situation I can imagine you getting into. The healings will just take longer without her. It's what I can't imagine—and what you're particularly good at creating—that worries me. Then there's your age. Even if you choose to stay in your late twenties for all eternity, I'd still like to follow your real into old age just so you have some options."

Sere wasn't sure being perpetually young was a bad idea, but it would limit her ability to create cover identities and disguises. "You've made your point. I won't mess with your equipment unsupervised again."

"I'm always around. Show up in my lab, and wherever I am, the security sensors will tell me you're here. I can work the equipment remotely, so you won't have to wait on me if things are dire. And Joe has enough of a technological med kit in his cabin to work as a doppelgänger field hospital. Just don't fuck with the computers yourself. It's not safe for anyone."

Sere stood up from the metal table as her energy returned. "There's something else. I saw green sparks on the horizon. Seven of them. You were able to identify Monty when he escaped hell. Any ideas on these latest seven fugitives?"

She had never seen the professor turn so pale. "I'll start running some diagnostics," he said. "Monty was somewhat obvious. He just got up from his desk and walked out of the city. Since Montgomery Fisher hadn't performed those same actions in life, my sensors picked up the doppelgänger's inconsistency immediately. But that was the last time the alarms went off."

Fucking wonderful. "Now are you willing to listen to my concerns that someone is acting against us from the other side?"

"Let's not jump to conclusions. Glitches happen."

Tell me about it. Those body harvesters in hell are some big-ass glitches. She kept that thought to herself. Though she knew better, people had a way of discounting her dreams as nothing more than fantasy and didn't listen to the underlying warnings. But laying all of hell's demons on Professor Yates's shoulders wouldn't help solve the faulty computations. Sere needed the old scientist-inventor to stay sharp, not filled with self-recriminations.

"If there are seven new demons headed to New Orleans to kill their reals, it would be helpful to know who I'm supposed to protect."

He connected the spaghetti noodle of wires from the wall of computers to his laptop and sat in the old lounge chair. "I'll get right on it. I have to warn you, though—if they slipped past my fail-safes, they won't be easy to identify. This may take some time."

"If the new demons are anything like Monty, I'll only have a few days before they start raising holy hell."

Professor Yates stared at the cascading formulae, data, and personal files as if trying to meld with the computer. "I'll do my best."

She felt wobbly as she pushed off from the table. "If I promise not to touch your precious equipment, do you think I could crash in your back room? These connections always leave me a little fuzzy." Much as she hated sleeping, her body needed to acclimate to the recent changes before she faced Joe in combat training.

"Help yourself."

2

When Sere roused herself out of her uncomfortable sleep on the concrete floor well before dawn, the professor was still going at it on his laptop. He was so far gone into his virtual realm that she feared disturbing him. *I can't sit around here all day waiting for you to figure out what happened. Time to put this reconditioned arm through its paces.*

She quietly gathered her things and snuck out the front door without him ever looking up from his computer screen. The Triton started with a touch of backfire. The bike had not been on a good long run in months, and carbon had built up in the cylinders. *We both need to get clean from our addictions—mine alcohol, yours overly rich gasoline.*

The early-morning ride out to the swamp invigorated her body and soul. Being clear of New Orleans's incessant temptations and breathing in the clean smells of water and plants sobered her to the reality ahead. But moving into the city had been for the best. She would only have attracted the demons if she'd stayed so close to the hellmouth.

Not that it matters, apparently, she thought. *Since the professor didn't notice them, and those doppelmorons still figured out how to escape as easily as kindergarteners leaving the sandbox, there must be a superior intelligence working behind the scenes in hell.*

She'd have to dig deeper in her search for the mastermind behind the escapes. Before she'd be able to convince those who could help that the doppelgängers weren't finding their own way out of hell, Sere needed a lot more evidence.

When she pulled up to Joe's cabin, he was sitting on his front porch, sipping coffee. "You're late. I saw the green flashes."

She pulled off her leather riding jacket and held up her healed arm. "Sorry. Had a little accident last night."

He set his cup on the beer cooler beside his chair. "What do you need?"

My ass kicked. "To clear my head and reconnect to this body."

He got out of the chair and stripped down to his boxer briefs. "I'll grab my bag. We can train down near the water. Lose your weapons. I need to see what condition you're in."

To avoid destroying a perfectly good set of leathers, she also tossed her pants and halter top on the seat of her Triton. "Let's do this."

"AGAIN," Joe demanded.

After only an hour of intense combat, Sere stood hunched over with her hands on her knees. "I can't breathe."

"What are you, twelve?" Joe hadn't given in to her whining since she was a little girl growing up in hell. And the last time he had played into her hand, she'd managed a good kick to his knee, dislocating the joint.

She took a deep breath and bounded up from her crouched position to grab the cypress tree limb above her head. "At least I didn't have to deal with my blood's oxygen level back then." She swung her heel toward his chest, but she was much too slow. He grabbed her ankle with both hands and twisted her out of her perch. She fell with a loud splash into the swamp.

"The demons you'll be facing will have the same limitations you do. Understanding what oxygen deprivation does to your reflexes and ability to think will put you a step ahead. I'm not out here simply to teach you how to overcome your weaknesses—you have to experience the pain so you'll know how to maximize it in your enemies."

Yeah, yeah. Stop your preaching. I've heard it all before. She spit mud out of her mouth. "You make it sound like my doppelgänger brethren will be easier to fight than a normal human."

"You already know better than that, which means you're trying to distract me."

He was right. She flung a fistful of swamp grass at his face and lunged out of the reeds toward his legs like an alligator attacking its prey. She barely managed to grasp his foot as he leapt away from her attack. Continuing her forward charge, she brought him down hard, but she released her hold before any lasting damage was inflicted on his joints.

Instead of the counterattack she expected, he got to his feet and stood over her with his fists on his hips. "Now you're just boring me."

During training, mercy was seldom well received. "Look, old man. If you hurt me, I'll regenerate fast enough. You, however, could be out of commission for weeks if I turn all of my aggression loose."

"How about you let me worry about that. We're not playing out here. You start pulling your punches based on your opponent's skill level, and those demons will eat you for lunch. Come on, little girl. Do your worst."

He was goading her into embracing her doppelgänger instincts. From the age of seven, when she'd been trapped in hell without even her father to guide her, Joe and her other guardians had trained Sere to rely on her spiritual self as a way of containing the evil that came with her reproduction body.

"Stop testing me," she said.

"Come on, hellion. Let me have it. Pussy."

He was getting under her skin. The derogatory female label didn't bother her, but she hated that he was treating her like a child who could be easily manipulated.

"Knock it off, Joe. I'm warning you."

"*Warning* me?"

"You know what I'm saying. If I go all in and let go of my mental control, I won't be able to stop myself." The fear that she might not find her way back and become like every other doppelgänger had never been so pronounced.

He walked over to his field pack and pulled out his pump-action riot scattergun. She didn't need to be told what was loaded in the chamber. Even from ten feet away, the paranormal shell raised goose bumps on her arms. He set the weapon against the tree.

"Best to find out what you're capable of—and your limitations—out here in the swamp, where it's just the two of us, rather than down in New Orleans where the loas of the dead might get called in."

Joe had been more than just her instructor. *Father figure* wasn't a term she could embrace, but for twenty years, he'd been the one whose approval she most craved. She was torn between wanting to impress him and wanting to protect him.

"You couldn't shoot me even if I did go full demon on your ass."

He nodded toward the shotgun. "It's not a full load—just enough to dim your lights. Now, fight me like you mean it, or I'll shoot you just to piss you off."

A red tinge overlaid the swamp's rich colors of early morning like a tinted lens. It was as if all of Sere's education and conditioning had added layers of color to her perception of the world. She let go of her hold on reality, and the nuanced human emotions fell away, leaving increasing shades of anger. She attacked Joe with a savage fury she hadn't thought herself capable of.

But all of her youth, physical training, and agility were

countered by his cunning. Each gymnastic tumbling assault she made that should have resulted in a blow to his body was quickly parried with martial-arts moves, landing her facedown in the muck. The shades of red grew darker with every fall until all around her appeared as figures drawn in blood.

"Fucking shoot me, Joe!"

The old man was winded and hurt but undaunted. "Not yet. You're only fighting with half of your skills, *little girl.*"

Like a computer booting up in her skull, her wrath sought out her combat training. Her next attack, though still wild demon in nature, would be supplemented by everything Joe had taught her. *God, I hope I don't kill him.* Though she'd never had use for deities, for the first time, she hoped a higher power existed to save those she cared about from her.

She came at him much the way she had with her previous attacks, but once Joe had set up for his countermove, Sere somersaulted over his sweeping kick, landed with her legs wrapped around his shoulders, and spun halfway around his neck as if acrobatically twisting off the lid of a jar. With his head held precariously between her thighs, she grasped his forehead and leaned back to the point where his neck would snap.

Instead of feeling the satisfying bone separation that she both feared and craved, Sere fell backward hard against the trunk of a cypress tree. Joe's knee came at her face so fast she didn't have time to let go of his skull to protect her head from the blow. His knee hammered her head against the solid anvil of the trunk. The red that betrayed her lust for violence turned into the black of unconsciousness.

Sᴇʀᴇ ᴄᴀᴍᴇ to with a splitting headache. Memories of a dream involving Jennifer Cranston making lunch for her son Bobby didn't help. The woman had no culinary skills at all, which was quite the insult to someone raised in New Orleans. Sere's blurry vision slowly focused on Joe rolling up the technology-laced strip of cloth. A computer cord twenty feet long snaked out to his cell phone, which was at a safe distance from her zone of signal-distorting energy.

"How did you manage it?" she asked.

"Countering your death grip? I've still got my little tricks."

She rubbed the lump on the back of her skull. "I'm glad." The mental cobwebs had her shaking her head. "I was going to kill you. I really wanted to. You shouldn't have let me go that far into my primal hell-based instincts." She felt around for the shotgun holes but found no rivers of blood streaming through her side. "Thanks for not shooting me, by the way."

"I trust my training even if you don't. You weren't going to get permanently lost in that doppelgänger body. Now, tell me what you're really afraid of."

Battered from a training session, she was ready to answer that question. Truth was like an onion with layers that weren't always easy to access. She sometimes needed pain to help her get down to the core.

"Someone in hell was pulling Monty's strings," she said. "I'm certain of it. I don't think I can face a concerted attack alone."

"Have you considered that you may be getting a little paranoid? If there were some malevolent organization in hell, Professor Yates would have seen something on his computerized diorama. After all, it was his equipment that first identified Monty as a threat."

"He didn't notice the seven demons that escaped hell last night."

Joe gripped the barrel of his shotgun so tightly that Sere wondered if he was contemplating going on the hunt himself. "You could have led with that piece of information."

"Sorry. Your training sometimes proves overpowering. 'Never give out more information than needed, even to your allies.' I believe those were your words."

"What did the good professor have to say about our latest interlopers' covert escape?"

"He's working on it," Sere said, unable to hide her snarky disdain, especially from Joe.

"You don't trust him?"

"I trust him with my very existence. I kind of have to. But after my run-in with Thomas, I'm limiting how much I lay on that old man. I have my doubts about these puppet assistants he keeps creating. When it comes to those he works with, the professor is a little too free with information."

Besides, she thought, *the old man keeps limiting my powers. Why do all these people think they need to control me?*

"I'm still not convinced this isn't just a caravan of lost souls. Maybe some hell tour bus took a wrong turn and ended up sinking into the swamp."

I wish, Sere thought. "Hell's gate isn't so easily accessed. I have Lefty swimming around, doing guard duty out in the swamp. With any luck, that big ol' gator took out a couple of my adversaries, but that's not an outcome I can rely on."

Joe's eyes took on the cold, emotionless stare that indicated he was considering all options. "Assuming you're right, what was the point in sending only one combatant the first time?" His military training was kicking in.

"I think Monty was a test—basically a proof of concept. My adversary would have known I crossed over. He would have tried to recreate my success but without knowing what the limitations were. He probably thought only one being could cross over at a time."

Joe sucked on a blade of grass while leaning against the tree next to his shotgun. "Or he wondered what would happen to his test subject when he did make it out of hell. Each time Kendell and her gang crossed dimensions, their new bodies were based on their souls. You came through the portal more or less unchanged, but again, you possess a soul, unlike the doppelgängers in hell. From your archenemy's perspective, there were a lot of unknowns. He might have feared creating a monster he couldn't control."

Sere had another worry—her enemy had to be able to watch the events in life. "Whoever's behind the screen must know I'm the one who killed Monty. I may have dissolved the doppelgänger and won the fight, but in doing so, I exposed my strengths and weaknesses."

Joe nodded. "A good leader learns from his soldier's defeats. You think this small task force is his next move against you? While Monty was here, you were pretty convinced he was just after Mr. Fisher."

He was right—she had not been outmatched by Monty. And combatting the doppelgängers individually, Sere still had a fair chance. But demons from hell without souls didn't concern themselves with fair play. If a group of them came after her, she had no strategy in place.

"I'm still convinced Monty's primary objective was killing his real and taking over the man's life. That was what my enemy was investigating—to see if it was possible. When I foiled Monty's attempt, I made myself the target for the lead doppelgänger. Ultimately, I still think the demons that make it through the gate want to take over the lives of their living reals. They can't do that if I'm constantly sending their sorry asses back to hell."

If she was right about the number of combatants being dependent on the number of people the doppelgängers killed, that team could continually refresh and grow with every new murder. On her side, she knew fewer than a dozen humans she could rely on, and each of them was far too easily damaged. Other than Joe Cazenave—and possibly Bart the meddlesome bartender—not one of her people was good in a fight.

"How can you turn that knowledge to your advantage?" Joe asked.

"An army means a chain of command, and that means whoever is behind the breach between dimensions has to trust others. I don't have to worry about coordinating my efforts. Whatever force came through the gate last night doesn't have the capacity for independent thought. The more of them there are, the easier they'll be to defeat, because the one in charge will have his hands full operating so many drone doppelgängers. And if he loses control of his squad, they'll individually head down to New Orleans to fulfill their primary purpose of taking over the lives of their reals. There are only so many routes from the swamp to the city. Those doppelidiots' homing instinct will give me a goal to defend."

"If it were you planning the attack, would you opt for small groups of coordinated skilled assassins or a military platoon?"

I'd go alone, she thought, but admitting her recklessness to Joe had a way of resulting in another intense training exercise to show her the folly of such an action. "I have the benefit of having you on my side. Fortunately, there's no Joe Cazenave doppelgänger for my opponent to call on."

"Why do you think I spend so much time in this godforsaken swamp?" Joe said.

"Hey, this is my adopted home you're talking about. Without skilled teams, I would expect brute force over hidden snipers. If I can isolate each soldier, my odds are pretty good. If they bum-rush, however, I'll have my hands full. My four-barrel shotgun only holds four shells, and a single shot isn't likely to drop a full-grown doppelfucker."

"Then why not send a dozen doppelgängers or a hundred? He's got demons to spare."

"Monty murdered seven people on his killing spree. You were the one who taught me not to believe in coincidences." She had to share that. Joe needed the complete picture to run his analyses.

Joe let out a long, low whistle. "Interesting. I'm no expert when it comes to hell's rules. When you see your aunt

Kendell again, don't play cagey with that piece of information."

Who says I'm going to see her? Sere thought, but she knew better than to get in an argument with Joe over the obligatory family visits. "The connection is still just a theory. I'll continue watching the horizon each night."

"If you're right, these seven outlaws from hell would likely pick up where Monty left off. The more dead people, the more openings from the beyond." Joe fell silent as if his thoughts were taking him somewhere he didn't want to go—and worse, didn't want to share.

"Then I'll just have to stop them before they get frisky." She enviously eyed his riot gun. "Too bad that thing only fires one shot at a time and is so damn big."

"I've never known you to rely on guns. You've got your combat knife and hand-to-hand training. Ultimately, those are what you need most. Just don't underestimate your opposition. A semiorganized band of mercenaries only needs to distract you long enough for one of them to get in a well-aimed shot."

Hopefully, whatever they were using as ammunition wouldn't be as deadly as the paranormal shells from hell that she had stashed in the ammo belt laid over her saddlebags. She also had Joe's secret stashes, although she only knew the location of a couple of them. He'd designed each of his caches to be accessed in cases of emergency, and they weren't just filled with weapons.

"If things get ugly, I could sure use access to a field med kit," she hinted.

Joe rolled up the computer cable and put it back in his

backpack. "No dice. Professor Yates informed me about your little break-in. Besides, you'd need a cellular connection. If you get hurt so badly you need immediate attention, there's no way you could set up the phone. I will, however, give you my human medical supplies. If you get shot or knifed, stem the bleeding, get word to me, and trust your skills." Joe rummaged through his pack for the nearly useless medical kit.

Sere began to see red. *Why won't anyone do what I ask? I had an easier time in hell.* "Fine. Don't give it to me. I'll just stay on a fifty-mile leash from you. Much farther than that, it's unlikely you'd reach me in time with that vintage motorcycle of yours." She glared at him, hoping he'd get more anger from her stare than from her words.

He snickered, which only further enraged her. "I can just see you. The snarling dog at the end of her leash, barking and threatening everyone beyond her reach. How about that bartender of yours? He's witnessed you heal enough times not to be freaked out by your unique anatomy."

He's seen enough of my body already, she thought. She didn't want to rely on Bart, but at least he was mobile. His Ducati Monster could reach her a hell of a lot faster than Joe's BSA Spitfire.

"I'm not crazy about the idea, but if that's the best you've got, I'll take it." *And con Bart out of the kit later.*

"I'll see that he gets it and knows to keep it handy at all times." Joe put the mostly useless human medical equipment in an oilcloth satchel. "You know, there is an alternative to going on the hunt. You're welcome to stay at my cabin for as long as you want. If you're right about them coming after you, there's nothing wrong with facing an enemy from a well-fortified defense."

Her head still hurt, but at least she was able to stand up. "Weren't you the one who taught me that sitting in a bunker was like being a crawfish in a pot? Eventually, someone always comes along and sets a fire under your ass."

Joe handed her the waterproof pouch. "This situation is slightly different. Being prepared isn't the same as hiding. But if you're so afraid of being trapped, I'll gas up my BSA and ride with you. Someone having your back might not be a bad thing. You don't have to face this alone."

I can't risk you getting hurt, but admitting her fear for his safety wouldn't go over well. "Can't have you slowing me down, old man. Besides, I'll need you to run interference on any police reports between the Northshore and New Orleans that might draw attention to me."

He retrieved his well-used pump-action shotgun. "Just the same, I'll be ready if you need me."

*a*fter a day of combat training, the ride on her motorcycle through the humid air and shadowy light of dusk calmed Sere's adrenaline-fueled nerves. Fighting required her to be focused only on the threat directly in front of her. Such all-encompassing attention, once satisfied, had a way of busting loose the logjam of potential dangers to reveal the strategies available to her. She headed north toward where she'd seen the green light show.

Someone in hell had it out for her. Of that she was certain, even if those around her weren't yet convinced. As she'd won the last round against Monty, her nemesis must have upped the stakes. That meant the seven doppelfuckers that corresponded to the green fireworks weren't just demon frat boys out for a night of terror on Bourbon Street. They were coming after her.

Then there were the loas of the dead to consider. They

were a constant looming threat, like a shadow whose source she couldn't identify. If there was an increase in doppelgänger-on-human murders, the guardians of the divide between life and death would get suspicious. All of her fighting skills wouldn't do a damn bit of good against spirits whose intent was to retrieve her soul from the living. At least in New Orleans she had people who understood and might be able to intervene, but running for safety wasn't going to stop the demon apocalypse.

She leaned hard into a right turn and twisted the throttle. "I can't do my best if I'm constantly worrying about those loa-life assholes. They're immortal. I'm immortal. We're just going to have to figure out a way to coexist." The words, however, only gave her a momentary sense of bravery. "The best way to keep the loas off my tail isn't to turn and run. I have to make a stand against those doppelshits up here, where I can better control the aftermath of dead bodies—real and fake. Stopping the human carnage before it gets started has to be my number-one aim. Even if I can't dissolve the demons, maybe I can convince these rural hicks to be on the watch for strangers in their towns."

Sere pulled into Riley's all-too-familiar gravel parking lot and shut down her café racer. Bart's establishment, Bubba's Bar and Grill, was still a good twenty miles down the road, but getting into a bar fight with his customers might not be the best way to enlist the obnoxiously hot bartender's cooperation. The gator hunter's bar, however, was an all-too-convenient place for Sere to work out her aggressions. Combat training with Joe involved skill and cunning—bar brawls were far less mentally taxing and much more fun. Between bar regular Cody, whose boat she'd borrowed without permission and truck tires she'd slashed, and Riley, who'd managed a well-aimed rifle shot into Sere's leg, she was assured a hostile greeting. Plus, taking on a bar full of drunk assholes to relieve the stress of the long ride beat showing up at Bart's with her unresolved emotions.

She unbuckled the holster of the four-barrel sawed-off shotgun and laid it over the rattlesnake-protected saddlebags. The blaster might prove too daunting even for the aggressive bar dudes. A rattling from within the gator-skin panniers indicated that her snakes weren't happy about her entering a fight so lightly armed.

"Relax. Joe might be able to knock me on my ass, but I've yet to be beaten hand to hand by a group of drunken rednecks." She checked the butt of her knife, which projected beyond the top of her boot. "I have what I need."

She pushed her way through the door like an Old-West gunman ready for a showdown. Unfortunately, Riley was ready for her. As soon as the door closed behind Sere, the curvy bar owner in skimpy jean shorts and a tiny T-shirt stepped out from behind the bar with her rifle at her hip, aimed at Sere's stomach.

"I expected you'd come back eventually."

Sere made her customary quick scan of the premises. As Riley was standing front and center, holding a weapon, she was first up for Sere's evaluation. In spite of the casual way Riley held the gun, the barmaid had proven her marksmanship when she'd plugged Sere's leg on a moving motorcycle from fifty feet away. But the woman had also lent Sere her boat to go after Monty. Riley's loyalties could be fickle that way. If Sere could provide some entertainment, the bar owner might back off to watch the show. A good brawl had to beat cleaning a pool of blood off the rough-hewn wooden floor.

Camo Boy Cody hadn't even changed chairs, let alone clothes, since their last encounter. The linebacker-turned-alcoholic still had muscle mass going for him but lacked the brains to use it beyond ramming into people.

Lurking in the shadows near the jukebox was a dude more intent on his date than on the confrontation. The girl pushed her hand against his chest as though playing hard to get, but based on the white cutoffs that crept up her ass cheeks and the halter top thin enough to display her rock-hard nipples, Sere guessed that her date wouldn't take the protest too seriously. If the couple joined in the fight, it would be merely because they were trying to get out the front door and into his truck before the cops showed up and checked on the girl's ID.

Behind Sere, a guy who fashioned himself as the bar bouncer leaned against the front door with folded arms. That much of a cocky attitude invariable resulted in a guy being more concerned about his junk than physical aggression in a bar. Sere calculated that he was only helping Riley out in an attempt to get into her skintight cutoffs. *Poor misguided fool. I'll bet that woman has an iron-grip vagina strong enough to snap your sniveling cock clean off like a rabbit's foot in a bear trap.*

She tried not to stare at the remaining guy at the bar,

who was slightly hidden by Cody's massive frame. The man was dressed as a member of the road-construction crew, but his movements were too precise for someone who'd spent the day doing hard labor. *Fuck!* The doppelgänger's skin hadn't turned translucent yet, but he was far too pale to pull off the outdoor look.

Sere's observations took a split second. She'd completed her assessment before Riley could spit out her next wad of chewing tobacco. "Looks like you've got a new customer," she said.

"Thanks to you. Cody picked him up out in the swamp just this morning." Riley lowered her aim to Sere's feet. "I wouldn't want to interrupt the night's entertainment—just wanted you to see that you're stuck here until I say otherwise."

"Always the classy lady."

Riley kept eye contact with Sere but leaned her chin over her shoulder to yell to the room, "Whoever knocks this skanky bitch on her ass drinks free for the rest of the night."

Sere gave Cody her squinty snake-eyed stare. The tub of flesh slunk away to the back room. Being bitten by a rattlesnake wasn't the kind of thing he was likely to forget, even drunk. *Not bad. One down before the fight even commences.*

Sere heard the chair scrape against the floor behind her. *Your opening move is far too obvious and loud. Clearly, you're not very experienced at bar brawls.*

She dove for the floor, leaving Bouncer Boy nothing to hit with his swinging chair. He whirled around from the momentum and crashed through the door he'd been

33

protecting. *Two down. Looks like it's just you and me, assgänger.*

She made a quick check of the dark corner to assure herself that the two lovebirds had chosen a less antagonistic form of physical exertion. With the dude's hands clasped tightly to the girl's firm breasts and her fingers exploring the top edge of his belt like a snake charmer teasing a cobra out of its basket, neither was in a position to join the fracas.

Riley had retreated to the area behind the bar but held her rifle over her shoulder as if expecting Sere to make a run for it. *Fat chance,* Sere thought. *I am seriously looking forward to the day I rip that gun out of your hands.*

But Riley could wait. First, Sere had to deal with the demon from hell. She turned to the big guy at the bar. "I'll wager you aren't from around these parts."

The burly blue-collar worker rose from his barstool, holding an empty beer bottle like a billy club. "Prepare to die."

"Not much for small talk, I see." *I need to get this moron between Riley and me so she doesn't have a shot.* Sere held her arms out wide. "Okay, fuck puppet. Show me what you've got." She circled away from the front door while planning her strategy. Though the patrons of the bar would be too drunk or distracted to believe what they were seeing, Riley's eagle-eyed stare would be sure to catch any strange healings from her new champion.

Sere backed into the cold metal rim of the round tabletop, which she felt through her leather pants. She consulted her mental inventory of the bar's furniture. *Cheap-ass round wooden tops over smaller barrels that look like someone tried to fit the wrong-sized top on a mason jar.* She edged her bottom along the lip until her foot encountered the cast-iron barstool. *Make your move, doppelfucker.*

The demon closed in toward her, blocking off Sere's view of Riley behind the bar. *Perfect.* Sere spun away from her attacker, grabbed the lip of the table with both hands, and flung it at him. It spun like some medieval Frisbee. The doppelidiot ducked but not low enough, and the wheel of death's metal rim skidded off the top of his head and knocked him to the floor.

No problem. That was just decapitation attempt number one. Using her foot, Sere heaved the heavy metal stool up into her hands. The demon struggled back to his feet and dropped his bottle.

"Here, let me help you with that headache." Sere let him have it with the barstool. The thick cast-iron base cleaved his head in half. Blood spread from his brainless skull, covering the wood-plank floor like red paint from an overturned five-gallon bucket. She increased her grip on the chair. An eyeball rolled out of what had been his head, but too much of the skull was still attached. Sere couldn't risk him regenerating. Hoping to look like some jilted lover who'd finally gotten even, she took an overhead swing of the cast-iron base and guillotined the mangled remains.

One doppelgänger decapitated in public. Not the best result but better than having these people see a demon come back to life. If I stick around, though, I might have authorities from both the living and the dead all over my ass.

Sere tossed the bloody stool through the window behind her. Like a superhero leaving the scene, she turned, launched off the wooden-barrel table base, and flew through the opening in the wall. With one gymnastic tumbling jump, she kicked the starter lever and landed on the back of her motorcycle.

Riley burst through the front door with a rifle in her hand just as Sere let go of the clutch and gunned the motor. "I don't give a flying fuck who you are or what you think you're doing," the bar owner yelled over the sound of the motorcycle's squealing back tire. "Show up around my bar again, and my boys will be the least of your worries. This is your final warning."

At least that bar bitch isn't shooting me this time.

BETWEEN THE SMELL of burnt oil and the sound of the backfiring engine, Sere didn't have to guess which direction Cody's truck had lumbered off in. She turned her motorcycle down the dirt road toward the swamp. *Do you ever go anywhere other than your boat and the bar? I swear, you must spend all of your time on either the thwart or the stool.*

Like a slow-moving turtle trying to outswim an alligator, Cody's truck was no match for Sere's motorcycle, though the cloud of dust and smoke did have both her and the Triton gasping for air. Halfway down the access road to the swamp, Cody turned onto an even narrower two-rut road that cut through grass tall enough to brush the undercarriage of his truck. Based on the grunge that coated Sere's boots as she followed him through the field, she guessed this was a route the truck took often. When the racket of banging metal and poorly tuned engine ceased, Sere pulled off the road and hit the kill switch. She doubted the idiot had anything worth worrying about, but this was his home turf.

Best to be prepared. She reached into her saddlebags and let the two snakes slither up her arms. Before walking the remaining way to the run-down cabin, she double-checked her shotgun to be sure it was fully loaded. He'd brought one doppelgänger in from the swamp. Where there was one, there could be more.

As Cody reached for the handle of the torn screen door, Sere pulled her knife and flung it at his wrist. She only missed by a few inches, impaling his arm and tacking it to the doorframe.

"Fucking whore!" He pulled the blade out of his flesh and cradled his arm like a little sissy.

"For an ex-football player, you sure aren't good with pain," she said.

"Most people knock on the door when they want something. They don't skewer the owner like a chunk of meat for the fire."

Sere spread her arms, and the two snakes crept out to her wrists, lifted their heads, and hissed ominously at Cody. "I couldn't be sure you didn't have another guest in the house like the guy at Riley's."

"Did you ever consider simply asking someone a question without first inflicting bodily injury?"

"Like you'd just tell me the truth without the threat of retaliation hanging over you."

"Retaliation involves harm *after* the offense, not before. *Pretaliation* isn't a thing."

This isn't getting me anywhere. He's probably stalling to give the demon in the cabin a chance to strike. She draped one of the snakes around her neck and pulled her shotgun out of its holster. "Consider it incentive. Lie to me, and we'll conduct our interview as we did last time."

He kept his hand on his arm to prevent blood loss and lifted it in protection against the snake. "For the love of God, woman, what do you want?"

She felt like she was talking to a toddler who was being intentionally difficult. "Is there anyone in that cabin?"

"No. The guy you killed at Riley's was the only one."

It's never that simple. "So you just gave him a ride into town out of the goodness of your heart?" she asked. "That doesn't sound like you."

"I swear, have you no sympathy for people at all? It's only good manners to rescue some fool who got lost. What did you expect me to do—leave him for gator food?"

She looked Cody over for any sign of deception. The man, wounded and unarmed, wasn't clever enough to lie. "I think we both know that dude at the bar was no innocent lost soul. I just want to know where you found him and if there were others with him."

Cody straightened up as if she'd pushed him as far as he intended to let her. "I'm not giving you any fucking ride back out on the water."

Again, she wondered why he couldn't simply answer her questions like an adult instead of a naughty boy constantly looking for a way out. "Where did you find him?"

Cody looked about to pass out. "At least let me get a bandage for my arm first."

Nice try, asshole. "Answers first." She aimed the gun at the door just in case there was someone inside.

"Fine, but it's not like there's a map of the swamp or signs at every river inlet. There's a reason people get lost out there."

The smile that touched only the corners of his mouth and slightly crinkled the edges of his eyes told Sere he hoped she'd end up as one of the lost. *Fuck. He'll probably just give me bullshit directions.*

"You've gotta get out past the hunting grounds, through the grove of old cypress," he continued. "Not the secondary-growth forest, but the really old trees. You know what I'm talking about?"

Duh. I spent most of my life out there. "I'm familiar with the area."

"I'm not surprised. The place is creepy as hell. Only a swamp witch would feel at home out there. Deep in that river jungle is a bottomless pond that has no business being there. It's almost as if someone has dredged the area looking for something. Crystal-clear water isn't natural in the bayou. I found that guy sitting against a tree, looking out on the water like some damn idiot."

"Could you find the spot again?"

Cody scampered back against the door of his cabin. "I told you before, I'm not your bayou tour guide. I swear, that's all I know. Now, can I please wrap this knife wound?"

"Toss me my blade first. If you're lying to me, my snakes might pay you a little midnight visit."

He heaved the combat knife halfway out to her. "Lady, I swear to God, I'd tell you anything just to never have to see you again."

SERE RODE through town at a leisurely pace. One brawl resulting in a killing was more than enough incentive for the cops to hunt her down. She didn't need to add a speeding ticket to the charges. Riley wasn't going to make a fuss and risk having her bar shut down as a crime scene, and no one was going to mourn a soulless puppet. Just the same, people talked. Sere needed to get out of there and focus on the dangers ahead.

The doppelfuckwads were moving fast. To stay on top of them, she was going to need updates on the goings-on in the little out-of-the-way bars. There was only one person along the winding highway that bordered the swamp who might listen. *Bartender Smooth, I guess one day I should learn your real name.*

The twenty-mile ride gave her just enough time to think. She hadn't hesitated in decapitating the doppelgänger in Riley's bar, but there were ramifications to consider. Monty's beheading had resulted in his real, Mr. Montgomery Fisher, being possessed by his evil double. The two had already met, however. Professor Yates had been clear that such a meeting between doppelgänger and real could have unfortunate consequences, and possession was one of them. Plus, Monty was killed in Mr. Fisher's presence, making the transfer that much easier.

The only other possession Sere had encountered was that of Professor Yates's original lab assistant, Thomas. *I was a child, and that doppelgänger hybrid never should have been created in the first place. I know Thomas blames me for the demon inside him, but his case was unique.*

Based on the two previous beheadings, Sere was fairly sure that Riley's doppelidiot would have only transferred an unexplained hangover to his real. Decapitation was more satisfying than blasting one of these carnival silhouettes with her shotgun. Still, Sere needed to at least get his name for her journal. It was still possible that in some dive bar, a passed-out road worker would wake up with deadly desires and killer instincts. If so, she had to be prepared.

I'll ask Bart to probe Riley on what she knows. The road made a long gentle uphill curve out of town. Sere was riding the same hill she'd coasted down to Kelly's Diner a couple of months before. *Don't think about her. She and Larry are together at last.*

She needed to stay focused on what she'd learned. If there was a weakness in her paramilitary training, it was the ingrained expectation that her opponent had a similar skill set. Riley's doppelidiot proved that wasn't the case. This wouldn't be the well-orchestrated attack she'd feared at Joe's—it would be a bunch of random bar-brawl cage matches. And if Sere didn't show up for the events, the devilish demons might raise holy hell with whomever they found just to get her attention.

Must be difficult corralling a group of soulless idiots let out of hell like college students on spring break. The one constant is that all these doppelhomies will be headed to New Orleans to confront their reals and party like the damned—killing randomly as they go.

She swung the Triton around the curves that cut through the forest. The roadway displayed by her headlight took on the familiar red tint that indicated she was letting her emotions get the better of her. Thinking about soliciting help from Bart had that effect on her. He always seemed to catch her at her worst and most exposed. At least she'd be able to make her petition fully dressed this time. Just once, she wanted to catch him with his pants down and in need of her help. But today wasn't going to be that day.

Her stomach felt like it was in her throat as she pulled into the gravel parking lot of the western-style saloon, and as much as she hated to admit it, the sensation wasn't the result of the hard ride. *Get your fucking hormones in check. He's nothing special. He's just a bartender. I could teach Lefty how to open beer bottles.* Unfortunately, Bart had more going for him than just a mixologist's sinewy forearms. Sere envisioned his dark-brown eyes, Navy SEAL tattoo, and riding leathers so skintight she didn't have to use her imagination to know he had dimples on the sides of his butt.

The picture in her mind made it hard to control the motorcycle between her legs. She rode past the row of Harleys and parked directly in front of the door. If things went badly—and they always seemed to with the biker crowd—she'd need a quick exit.

She swung her leg off the bike but held onto the handlebars in case her legs were still paying attention to the hormone-driven desires and not her commands. Checking the four-barrel shotgun holstered at her thigh helped her focus her attention on the threat of a fight that loomed when she entered the bar. With one look at the belt filled with extra shells that hung low on her hips, anyone would think twice before crossing her. But then, drunken bikers didn't always pay attention to much beyond her bare midriff and female curves.

She reached into her saddlebags and pulled out her two rattlesnake companions. "You guys keep bitching that you don't get to participate in all of the fun. This time, you can announce my presence."

She tossed the two vipers under the swinging bar doors. Startled screams of men greeted her companions. Satisfied that the men inside were sufficiently cowed, she pushed her way into the bar, wielding her shotgun. As she'd expected, most of the patrons had scrambled off their stools and were headed for the back wall.

"I'm not here to fight this time."

Bart didn't even put down the glass he was wiping clean. "Overcompensating much? Or do you just insist on making an entrance?"

She set the barrel of the shotgun over her shoulder. "I thought it might be nice to *not* bust up your bar for a change. I need your help."

He set aside the glass he was polishing and pulled down a bottle of Jameson's from behind him. "Sounds serious."

The bar customers huddled around the pool table as if they'd all decided they wanted a game. *Fucking male egos*, she thought as she watched the men pretend the snakes didn't bother them in the presence of a woman. Just to ensure that their mistress wasn't disturbed, the two vipers slithered their protective barricade ten feet past the end of the bar.

Sere sat at the polished cypress counter and accepted the shot of whiskey. "One of Monty's friends showed up at Riley's. I have reason to believe he wasn't the only one. This isn't a fight I can face alone."

Bart pulled out a second shot glass for himself. She'd never seen him drink. He filled the glass but left it sitting on the bar. "I assume you dispatched him with your typical flair. Is that earlier fight why my establishment is being spared your usual drinking habits?"

His attitude didn't help her maintain control of her desire for action. "Don't make me draw this out. Shit's about to get real. I beheaded that idiot in front of Riley and her barflies. There wasn't a way to dispose of the body, so I have to assume I'm about to have the cops up my ass. Any chance your cousin can tell us who he was?"

"I thought Joe was your connection with the police. Can't he stymie the investigation?"

"If we were simply talking about word of a bar brawl in a tavern on the Northshore getting down to the New Orleans Chief of Police, sure," Sere said, "but a homicide in front of multiple witnesses isn't so easy to sweep under the rug."

Bart downed his shot and returned the empty glass to the bar in one fluid motion. "I can see that. From what I hear, Sheriff Newton still hasn't let go of the last murders in this parish. With a new one to take care of, he'll put every available officer on the case."

Having sirens blast at her each time she gunned her motorcycle through a local town wasn't going to make finding the demons who were the true threats any easier. "I can't patrol the whole swamp on my own. You've seen what these assholes are capable of. It only took Monty a couple of days to figure out how to kill people without having the bodies splattered all over the place. Multiply that rampage times seven—well, now six."

The expression in Bart's wide, beautiful brown eyes from under his thick black eyebrows made it clear he didn't like the idea of his bar turning into a stopover for serial killers. "This is a sleepy little town on the bayou, and the killings piling up around here are not business as usual. If you're intent on beheading more demons, the cops aren't just going to look the other way while you add to the body count."

"Riley's idiot will be an ongoing problem, but investigations take time. Any doppelgänger who emerges from the swamp will have their real in New Orleans, and that means any investigation up here will undoubtedly rely on information from the big city. Joe might not be able to stop every police report in this little parish, but he can slow down the transfer of requests between departments. And even if Riley and her customers can come up with a unified description of me—which I doubt, due to their inebriated states—it's not like anyone is going to be able to look me up online. Joe taught me not to leave a paper trail regarding my identity."

"So you expect me to help you dispose of the bodies?" he asked.

She wondered if he'd go to that extreme for her. "I'm not looking for that level of trust. Not yet at least."

"That was some pretty weird shit I saw out in the swamp —two guys who could have been twins if one of them still had skin. As long as I live, I'll never forget how you decapitated that ugly bastard and called him a demon. From your intensity, I knew you weren't just being metaphorical. And based on his appearance, I'm inclined to give you the benefit of the doubt on that assessment. Then the Pleistocene Gator that's supposed to be pure myth swims out of the swamp, and a horde of snakes transfers the bloody remains onto its back. That's the kind of story that could end up with me being the village laughingstock."

"Let's not forget me healing right before your eyes."

"Twice." He refilled their glasses. "I'm willing to place my bet on you being the badass heroine and not the psycho serial killer, but I'm not going all in just yet."

"That's fair. I'm not asking you to go blowing demons' heads off."

"Just shoot their bodies once you're done decapitating," he said.

"About that. Apparently, you were supposed to shoot the head, not the body. But thanks for trying."

He stared at her with his penetrating eyes for an uncomfortably long time. "You have to be kidding me. How could it possibly matter?"

She couldn't see any reason to hide the full truth. "Monty was Montgomery Fisher's evil doppelgänger. Because the two of them had met and were in close proximity to each other when Monty was extinguished, his presence transferred into Mr. Fisher. The shotgun pellets were supposed to sever that connection, but with his head cut off, shooting the body only managed to blow it into a bloody pulp."

"Yeah. That would have been useful to know before I pulled the trigger."

She knew the feeling all too well. "The pip-squeak who delivered the bullets was a little short on information. There's no handbook on killing demons."

Bart eyed the bottle of Jameson's like a recovering alcoholic who'd already slipped two drinks off the wagon. "So that sweet CPA is now possessed by a demon?"

"It's not that simple. Technically, Mr. Fisher is not possessed, as the demon was based on the man himself. Think of it as more like personal desires he's trying to resist."

Bart turned his glass upside down on the counter. "I'm familiar with the temptation. So any demon you kill will have the same effect on some unsuspecting person in New Orleans?"

"No. If the doppelgänger and its real don't meet, the transfer can't take place."

"*Real?*"

"Sorry. The *real* is what we call the real person who acts as the blueprint for the doppelgänger's existence."

Again, Bart stared at Sere as if trying to see down to her soul. "You said Monty could heal just like you can. What's your connection to these demons?"

Bart had seen her naked, hurt, and on the hunt and had watched her body quickly heal, but some things were still hard for Sere to admit. She tossed back her shot for courage. "I'm one of them."

For a moment, she thought Bart was about to succumb to his temptation to fill the shot glass again. "Come again?"

"Look. It's complicated, and I've already wasted enough time. Are you going to help me or not?"

"You know, one day I'm going to meet a woman who says her story is very simple and easy to follow. I'm looking forward to that day. You do realize I have a bar to run. That last little adventure had me shut down for days."

She ran her fingers over the smooth butt of the shotgun at her side. "Bullshit. I've seen your waitress in action. She didn't have any problem clocking that pool player over the head with an empty beer bottle when things turned ugly last time. And I'll bet anything Fat Fuck over there never left his barstool during our little ride down to New Orleans. He may not be worth much, but he'd never let his favorite watering hole go belly-up. Besides, you know you loved the action."

The Navy SEAL tattoo on Bart's bicep waved like a flag in the wind as he flexed his muscles. "I've never turned away from a little danger."

She favored him with a smile. "Thanks."

"For what?"

"For not saying 'I've never turned away from coming to the aid of a damsel in distress.'"

His laughter made the butterflies in her stomach fly straight up to behind her eyes, making it hard to see clearly. "Darlin', I don't think anyone would consider you a weak female in need of rescue. Any dude who had the effrontery to do that would find his testicles dangling off the point of your knife."

She lowered her gaze to the bulge in his tight black jeans. "You've got that right. So I can count on your help?"

"I wasn't kidding about needing to run this place. Even with the help of my regulars, there are chores than need doing. I can't just jump on my bike and ride around after you. What exactly do you need?"

The prospect of having him with her on the hunt made the butterflies flap so hard she became lightheaded. "What I really need is information. Riley seemed to know who she was dealing with regarding that demon. I don't think it was mere coincidence that he found his way to her bar. But now that I've defeated one of them in a favorable fighting arena, future demons will likely show up just about anywhere. All I know for sure is they'll be oozing up out of the swamp. I need eyes and ears from here to New Orleans if I'm going to catch them before they go on individual killing sprees. I also need to know as much as possible about the doppelgänger I killed. Somewhere out there is the actual human, and I need to make sure he hasn't become possessed."

Bart nodded toward the two snakes, who—between their hissing and their rattling—were keeping his customers at bay. "You do realize siccing your vipers on those bikers isn't going to ingratiate them to your plight."

"Yeah, about that…"

"You want me to ask them, don't you?" He gave her a snarky look that she could have done without.

"You know I'd never back down from a fight, but as you surmised with the snakes, it won't help to intimidate those boys—and beating the shit out of them is probably not the most effective way of getting their help."

He pointed seductively at her leather riding pants. "How much money do you have on you?"

She never paid much attention to what kind of cash she had available. She reached into the impossibly tight pocket and pulled out a small handful of twenties. "Must be left over from what Professor Yates gave me."

"It'll do. Call off your snakes."

She turned toward the room and let out a low-pitched whistle. The two rattlers begrudgingly slithered away from the crowd and toward the door.

Bart snatched the money from her grip and held it high. "Next round is on the badass!"

Whatever fear the burly bikers might have had regarding Sere and her pets was overcome by the offer of free booze. Though they didn't shout her name and hoist her up on their shoulders, they did gather around the bar and appreciatively nod at her. Fat Fuck even made eye contact without adding a derogatory comment about her diminutive size and supposedly weaker gender.

After Bart prepared each of their favorite libations, he raised his still-empty glass to command the room's attention. "First, let's let bygones be bygones. The bar fight a couple of months ago was nothing new."

"Other than having a girl kick our asses," said Fat Fuck.

Bart nodded. "True, but my point is, we've all mixed it up a time or two. No reason to hold that against Sere."

Loud Mouth, who still had a fading black-and-blue mark on his jaw from where Sere had broken it during the brawl, slowly turned his bourbon and coke in his hand. "I'm getting the feeling this drink isn't as free as I was led to believe."

Bart added another shot of bourbon to the man's drink. "All we're asking is that you stay alert during your rides and tell me if you see anything out of the ordinary. Riley's bar had an unsavory character this afternoon. We can all respect a good bar fight, but ambushing a woman when she isn't prepared borders on abuse. I'd hate to see anything like that happen in my joint. And spread the word: anyone who finds this asshole's companions gets a free shot on me."

Fat Fuck pushed his beer stein back toward Bart. "I'll report back to you on anything I see." He barely cast Sere a sideways glance. "But I never want to see her skanky shadow cross the threshold of this bar again. Those are my terms. How can anyone enjoy a good beer when they're constantly at risk of snakes being hurled at them?"

A general murmur of agreement went up among the men.

4

*S*ere drove away from Bubba's, grateful to not have the drumbeat of a dozen Harleys chasing her ass. She had no delusions about the fat slobs lifting a single finger to help her should she run across a demon, but they'd never betray their favorite bartender. *Bart does have his uses. Though I'd never want to say that in his vicinity. That dude already has a big enough ego.*

Out on the road, she considered what to do next. With Bart's customers watching for strangers in the local taverns, she needed to again approach the gator hunters. They would likely be the first to make contact with the demons. This group, however, didn't include an intermediary bartender favorable to her cause—which left her to rely on her nonexistent charms. She would also need to find boaters who weren't patrons of Riley's.

I need a different approach. The true hunters are mostly

family men, not nightly bar patrons. I need to meet them where they'll listen to me.

At the road-construction camp, she turned away from the swamp and the long winding highway into the next town. Passing Kelly's Diner again was more than she could face. Monty had made it to shore by stowing away in the johnboat Sere had borrowed from Cody, and she would forever carry the guilt that for that. Then the demon asshole had followed her into town and killed Larry and Kelly. The memory ate at her like a slow cancer, getting worse each time she passed the diner. Even in the dead of night, she couldn't brave riding through town.

She had to stop as many demons as possible while they were still deep in the bayou, and that meant getting out on the water. After her last adventure, however, the gator hunters had gotten more diligent in patrolling their docks. If another boat did go missing, she'd be their first, and likely only, suspect—as if being wanted for murder wasn't bad enough. She needed the hunters on her side, not railing against her.

The meandering country road wound over a small hill that overlooked the back of Riley's poorly lit bar. Behind the shiplap shack, the rusted-out trailer that had cradled the bar owner's dilapidated boat still hung from the pine tree.

Sere pulled off the road to look over the swamp and consider what she knew. Cody had taken her out in Riley's beat-up boat to find Kelly and retrieve his johnboat from Monty. Once they found Cody's boat, he left Sere out there to face Monty alone. But after Monty killed Kelly, he took

Riley's boat to make his escape. That had left Sere with no other option than to swim her way out of the swamp.

If Riley's combination of rotting plywood, fiberglass, and outboard motor is still afloat, I might have my way back out to the deep swamp. Since the bar owner hadn't gone to fetch her boat, Sere doubted anyone was going to miss it.

But where is the damn thing? She could only clearly see the road below her for half a mile before the overhanging trees made the entire area look like one big forest. She restarted her motorcycle. Much as she loved the old bike, it wasn't much use when it came to searching the interconnected waterways, marshes, and sandbars that made up the swamp. When she reached the main road, she turned north—away from Riley's—and back toward the edge of town.

As far as Sere knew, Larry had no family to take over the business, so it was no surprise that his machine shop was boarded up. Eventually, some lawyer would figure out who was next in line to inherit the accumulation of tools and parts, but property law moved slowly in Louisiana. Without the loving brilliance of the master mechanic, the stuff would probably not be worth much anyway—certainly not enough to warrant the place being overly secured. No one was going to care if she snuck in.

Sere drove around to the back of the garage. *Dark and quiet* wasn't the shop's natural state. She longed to hear the tinny transistor radio accompanying the clanking of metal, tuning of engines, and squeal of grinders indicating that the tool monkey was pursuing his passion. A feeling of mourning now permeated the premises. Reverently, she picked the back lock with the tip of her combat knife.

The dark workshop gave her the chills. She'd never put much belief in inanimate objects holding residual emotions of the people who'd used them. She ran her fingers over a 9/16 open-end wrench on the workbench. In spite of her doubts, she could practically hear its desire to once again be of use in fixing some pesky problem.

"Someone needs to put this shop back in use as is. Breaking up all these tools would be a crime. I wonder how Joe would feel about having a real garage instead of all those makeshift cargo-container caches."

Though the idea of Joe having that much space to tinker on his motorcycles made her smile, she strongly doubted he would see the appeal of being so tied down to one spot. She pushed the Triton to a dark corner, covered it with a canvas work tarp, then jotted "Property of Joe Cazenave" on a work order and pinned it to the tarp. *Can't have someone selling that off by mistake.* Not that her rattlesnakes would let anyone within three feet of their mistress's possessions.

"I'd take you with me, but you two aren't fond of swimming. I'll find Lefty on my own this time."

The soft rattling from the bottom of the bags indicated that after their bar adventure, the snakes were just fine with hanging out and hunting rats in the old machine shop.

Unfortunately, Sere's favorite ancient gator wouldn't be the only creature from hell lurking in the uncharted area of the swamp. She pulled the blaster shotgun from her leg and turned it in her hands. "I wish I wasn't going to need you, but Joe would have my ass if I wandered into demon territory unprotected." She started rummaging around Larry's shop in search of some waterproof cloth she could form into a bag to keep her weapon and ammunition dry during her swim.

WHILE IN THE WORKSHOP, she changed into the black aquatic leotard she kept stashed in her saddlebag. After the swim through the swamp that had ended in her facing Bart naked on his dock, she'd made the skintight swimsuit part of her limited travel wardrobe. Nudity didn't bother her, but standing exposed and in need before the arrogant bartender had forced her to reconsider her swimming attire. She had to admit, the tight-fitting one-piece did work well for fighting.

With the combat knife sheathed against her thigh and waterproof-wrapped shotgun strapped across her back, she checked the fit in Larry's bathroom, pulling the leather belt tightly around her waist. The reflection in the mirror looked like some deranged, sexy, aquatic ninja. Not that any demon she might run across would care how she looked.

After a couple of quick combat poses to make sure she had sufficient maneuverability, she headed out the back door to sneak her way down to the swamp in her skimpy black outfit. Her water sandals didn't make a sound against the pavement. In an attempt to make her lily-white arms and legs blend in with the shifting shadows, she kept her movements in time with the breeze that swayed the tree limbs. *Next time, I need to remember to stash some black camouflage paint into my bag.* With any luck, people wouldn't be paying much attention to the goings-on outside their windows.

She scurried across the dimly lit street at the edge of town to the dirt road leading to the alligator hunters' docks. Without the need for a boat, she only followed the well-rutted access until she came to a walking path that presumably led to a secluded fishing spot. Lights from cabins that were nestled back among the trees helped illuminate the winding trail. When Sere got to the water's edge, she checked around herself to be sure she was out of sight of the small houses. Before entering the river, she tossed a small stick as far as she could into the stream. It quickly floated away in the opposite direction from the dock around the bend. *Perfect. The tide's going out.*

She eased into the warm water and let the current take her downstream. After he'd killed Kelly, Monty's next attack had been south along the highway leading to New Orleans. The boat he'd used had to be close to where he struck. Sere kept to the river's edge while searching every dark bend for the broken-down craft.

A mile from town, she spotted a glimmer of pale blue that bobbed with the current like a big fishing lure. With two strong breaststrokes, she approached the rounded engine housing that floated low in the water. She hoped the hull wasn't completely waterlogged.

In the filtered light of the full moon she could just make out the front of the boat beached alongside a fallen log. She reached underwater and grabbed the back gunnel. By tipping, pushing, and pulling the hull against the fallen tree, she managed to get the boat out of the silt and relatively empty of water.

She pulled the small craft off the shore and let it bob freely over her palms, like a mother protecting her child on her first swim. "Well, you float. That's something, at least."

As she climbed out of the water, she grabbed the rotting painter and jammed it under a rock. She shed the improvised backpack and unraveled it on the log. Though safer with the waterproof tarp around it, her shotgun wasn't going to do her much good if she had to take the time to unwrap it should a demon show his ugly face.

She strapped the holster to her leg and snugged up the bullet belt across her hips. With that and the knife at her other leg, she'd be ready for anything that might show itself in the dead of night. The tarp wasn't very big, but then, neither was the boat. She tossed it into the bow in case the splintery hull sprung a major leak, and she climbed on board.

The motor swung side to side as if saying, "Not gonna start. Not gonna happen."

She tugged hard on the starter cord, but true to its appearance, the motor stubbornly refused to kick over. "Look, I know you're an old curmudgeon, but being obstinate isn't going to do you any good. I'm betting you've got one good all-nighter left in you." She pulled again, but this time, the rope yanked back. "Fine. You asked for it." She popped one of the shotgun shells out of her belt and crushed the thin plastic coating in her hand. After opening the gas cap, she funneled the small paranormal pellets into the tank. *Hopefully, they're big enough not to get sucked into the carburetor. Let's see if they work on inanimate objects as well as they do on living animals.* She only had to pull the oxidized rubber handle halfway from the engine before it roared to life. "That's more like it."

She settled in against the back transom to keep the bow up out of the water and gunned the engine. There were no signposts for the gate to hell, and she'd told Lefty to remain on guard in case any other demons crossed over so it would be up to her to find him. In spite of Cody's directions, Lefty could be anywhere, and the chugging little boat probably didn't have six hours of gas left in its contaminated tank. *I just need to go far enough out there to get away from the gator hunters. This whole plan will go tits up if they spot Lefty before I can contact him.*

To Sere's surprise, the little boat lasted seven and a half hours before conking out for good. She opened the gas cap. All that was left in the rusted tank were her shotgun pellets rolling around in a layer of muck. She patted the peeling paint of the engine housing. "You did well, noble beast. But it looks like this might be your final resting place."

As the first rays of dawn filtered through the cypress trees, she got out and pulled the hull up onto the shore. The dilapidated skiff might still prove useful in marking the most recent access to hell's gate. "At least no demon is going to steal you to make their way back to civilization."

Turning back to the river, she pulled another shell from her belt. "Time to call in some help." She emptied it in her hand and spread the small pebbles out on the water. A flotilla of aquatic life answered her call. Bending down, she looked into the eyes of the fish and reptiles that swam just below the surface of the river. "Find the Pleistocene Gator. Tell him I need him." The little critters swam off in all directions.

It could be hours before Lefty answered her call. Her last attempt at restful sleep so close to the interdimensional gate had resulted in her doing battle with a harvester in hell. *Maybe I'll take a walk around the island this time.*

The dense mat of rotting vegetation squished under her feet. Insects scurried along with her as if welcoming her into their habitat. Rich smells of flowering plants, nutrient-laden water, and unseen animals calmed her mind. *I need to find a lookout post.*

Sere took a running start at the base of a tree that grew a few feet out into the river. She skipped along the tops of the cypress knees then launched herself high enough to grasp a lower limb. Then, by vaulting from branch to branch, she quickly ascended high above the swamp. On the highest branch thick enough to support her slender frame, she stood facing the open water beyond the cypress grove. From one hundred feet above the calm water, she'd be able to see any demon that might wish to sneak up on her.

She took the knife out of its sheath and held it high. "Any of you assholes want a fight, I'm right here!"

She returned her knife to its leather holster and sat on the thick limb with her back against the trunk, preparing for her vigil. Time in the swamp invariably reminded her of the angel who'd raised her—the person who'd opened her home and heart to a frightened and lost little girl. "I wish I knew what happened to you, Sanguine."

The woman who was more angel than human had sacrificed everything to remain in hell just to raise Sere. With her giant wings and insect-like eyes that could see the past and future, Sanguine Delarosa truly was Sere's guardian angel. But for all of her love for the strange swamp witch, Sere couldn't help feeling that Sanguine was falling down on the job.

"We had an agreement: I'd try life among real people, and you'd stand watch over the denizens of hell. How are these assholes getting past you?" None of the answers Sere came up with gave her any sense of peace, and she wanted to find Sanguine and ask her. Riding Lefty back to hell to find out what had become of her surrogate mother, however, would just leave the doppelgängers free to invade reality. Then they'd go on killing rampages before finally murdering their reals and taking over their lives.

Save the person I love the most, or stop the apocalypse. I know which one you'd choose. You'd never forgive me if I followed my heart and abandoned the living.

A flock of doves landed on the end of her branch. "Sanguine always said that if I was ever afraid, I should tell you birds, and you'd deliver the message. So here's what I want to say to her: I'm not concerned for myself. I've been well prepared. But I can't help wondering what happened to you, my beautiful angel. Just send me some sign that you're okay."

The birds flew off in the formation of an airborne feathered heart toward the deep swamp. As they disappeared from sight, Sere lowered her gaze toward the water, where distinctive ripples stretching from shore to shore indicated that Lefty had heeded her call. The rustling in the bushes behind him, however, told her that he wasn't alone.

I'll have to sacrifice my bird's-eye view for a more direct shot at Lefty's pursuer. Sere eased down to a lower limb. Positioned below the tree canopy, she hoped Lefty wouldn't notice her movements. If he caught sight of her too soon, he would rush to her like a puppy who'd just seen his mistress return home. The big goofy gator never noticed who or what was following him, only what was straight ahead.

She pulled out her shotgun and made sure it was fully loaded then cocked the upper two barrels. Joe was right: her aim sucked. *From this height, I should have a clear shot at the demonfucker without risking Lefty's hide. So long as my boy keeps swishing that giant tail, he should remain well ahead of whatever's following him.*

Even if by some chance the gator did get struck, it would take a lot more than a shotgun shell filled with paranormal rubble to take him down. "One cartridge will disrupt the signal to any creature weighing less than one hundred pounds," Andy, Professor Yates's latest hell-based assistant, had said. He hadn't given her much to go on when he'd delivered the bullets, but that limitation stayed at the forefront of her mind.

She closed her eyes to drive out the memory of being shot by Monty. *And that was only a handful of pellets.* The black spots on her side were a continuous reminder to keep clear of the damn stones.

Lefty burst into the open body of water below her, undulating his tail like the puppy she'd imagined. "Keep going. Don't stop." She lay flat on the tree limb and stared intently through the shotgun's sights at the reeds along the water's edge. "Come on, you asshole. Show yourself."

A young man burst through the trees on the opposite bank of the river. *He could just be some dumb teenager chasing Lefty. I need to be sure he's from hell*, she thought. Once he was close enough for the contents of the shotgun shell to do some damage, she could take action.

Her heart beat so hard that the end of the gun shook from the pulses. The water below her splashed against the shore, indicating that Lefty was swinging around. She kept her attention firmly planted on the kid running along the riverbank. He elbowed his way through a thick outcropping of hawthorn that grew at the water's edge. Red lines traced along his arm where the spikes had ripped at his flesh. She took careful aim and watched the bloodiest cut. It healed before he'd swung his arm free of the bush.

She took a deep breath and let it out slowly. When there was no more air in her lungs, she squeezed the trigger while keeping all of her focus on the kid running along the muddy shore. The pellets shredded the side of his T-shirt. Blood erupted through the white cotton. "Fuck. I only hit him with half the load."

The boy's face transformed into the demon she'd expected. With his bared sharp teeth, red eyes, and transparent skin, he looked up at her, intent on ripping her throat out. She cocked the remaining two hammers of her shotgun and took aim at the doppelfucker's stomach. She needed to land as many pellets with this shot as possible. Just as she pulled the trigger, however, he lurched into the brush as if yanked out of the way.

"Fuck!" Sere snapped the gun open to reload, but even as she forced the new shells into the barrels, she could sense the dead quiet on the other side of the river. "I know you're out there," she yelled. "Come out and face your demise." The reeds at the edge of the woods quivered. "Trying to escape?"

She fired off one of the chambers in an attempt to flush him out, but from the way the plants waved more than shook from the blast, she knew the demon was out of range. *Damn it. He's going to make me chase him.*

She jumped down from the tree and landed on Lefty's scaly back. "After him." With one long swing of his tail, he had her across the river. "This will go a whole lot easier on you if you'd just come out of those bushes," she shouted. "You don't belong here."

"Then where do I belong? Because it sure isn't hell. I didn't do anything to deserve damnation." Though filled with rage, the voice still carried the youthful high notes of the demon's real.

Sere was very familiar with the argument. No doppelgänger condemned to hell—including her—thought their fate was fair. "Not my call. Find some other dimension to escape into. This one's full."

"So you'd just let me go back the way I came?"

She crouched low in the brush, listening to every nuance of his voice as it filtered through the vegetation. *Gotcha. Just behind that young oak.*

"Nope. I'm sending you back without your body or memories. Don't worry—the professor's projection will regenerate you from scratch. I can't trust that you won't share with your demon buddies your knowledge of how to escape hell." The moment she stopped talking, she lowered herself to the ground, cocked two of the shotgun hammers, and crawled through the brush to a new position behind the tree. When she saw the back of the kid's muddy tennis shoes, she jumped to her feet, held the weapon at her waist, and blasted a hole a foot in diameter through the wounded demon's back.

She only caught a glimpse of the flying rock in her peripheral vision before it struck her in the side of her head.

WHEN SERE CAME TO, she was facedown in the dirt. She couldn't move her arms or legs. The vines tied around her wrists and ankles stretched out to the trees. Her knife stood with its blade facing down next to a cut creeper well beyond her reach. *Fuck.*

"All right. You've got me. Now what are you going to do?

We both know doppelgänger peckers are practically useless, so rape would just be an embarrassment for you."

"That's not what you said when we were kids."

She struggled against her restraints to get a look at her abductor. "Am I supposed to know you?" None of her liaisons in hell with the random sex puppets she'd found attractive had left much of an impression.

"I suppose sex with someone without a soul was less meaningful for you than it was for me—what with you actually having a soul. If that's what you want to call it."

Her back hurt from trying to contort her way around to face him. "If this whole demons-escaping-from-hell adventure is due to you feeling like a jilted lover, I really can't help you."

"Don't flatter yourself. I'm not the one who opened the door. You were. And I'm not the one who's standing in hell, holding the signpost showing my brothers and sisters the way out."

Then who is? Though I wouldn't believe you even if you did tell me.

"What do you want, then? Because if you signed up to escape hell just to tell me you love me, I might bust a gut laughing in your face."

"When we were kids and you started having your way with me, I was nothing more than an empty shell. At some point, though, I started seeing my existence as being unique. Sex with you wasn't about falling in love. It was about discovering my true self independent of my real."

Peachy. Now I'm responsible for making this fool self-aware. I'll bet this idiot thinks that qualifies as having a soul.

"You're still just an empty shell," she said. "Just because you can now see the glass, that doesn't mean there's anything in it."

"For someone who's tied up and defenseless, you've sure got a lot of spunk." He picked up her shotgun from where she'd dropped it and opened the barrel. "One load left." He closed it up, cocked the hammer, and aimed the weapon at her head. "I just witnessed what this thing can do to an empty glass. I wonder what would happen if you were on the receiving end. Do you think you'd land in hell or in Guinee? The loas of the dead might even offer me a reward. I think I'll ask for my real in return for their lost little girl. That sounds pretty reasonable to me. What do you think?"

Fear wasn't an emotion Sere accepted. Showing weakness had its place in drawing an opponent off guard, but actually breathing in that level of vulnerability implied that there was no way out. Besides, she'd already lived most of her life in hell, so that wasn't a meaningful threat. If she ended up in hell, she could finally help Sanguine out of whatever mess she was in. And as for the loas of the dead, they were only a problem if they ran across her while she was still alive.

"I'm kind of curious about what a full load would do to me as well." She arched her side so the leotard separated along her ribs, displaying the peppered black dots from Monty's shotgun blast. "So far, they've just left me with the beginnings of an interesting tattoo."

"You're so full of shit." He raised the weapon to his shoulder.

Sere held her hands to the ground as if that would help

quiet the rumbling under her body. Her former play toy was so focused on scaring her that he didn't notice what was racing up behind him. With one loud crunch, Lefty snapped his giant jaws closed around the doppelgänger, folding him in half like a taco. Only the end of the shotgun barrel protruded from the interlocking razor-sharp teeth.

"Drop it, Lefty. Drop! Bad gator."

The giant opened his mouth and let the crushed gun fall out. Blood and gore dripped from his teeth. Most of the doppelgänger's body was still intact but snapped in two like a twig. The demon's distorted face and wide red eyes still glistened with life.

"You're just damn lucky, mister. If that gun had discharged in your mouth, you'd be facing one killer set of cavities. Even in hell, I don't know of any vets willing to work on your ornery hide. Finish your treat, then come snap these lines. I hope you're hungry. We can't leave any evidence behind, and there's another doppelgänger morsel around here somewhere for you to clean up."

IT HAD ALREADY BEEN a long morning when Sere settled in between Lefty's broad shoulders for the daylong trip back to civilization. He kept his head high in the water and tail swishing with joy after his satisfying meal of two freshly caught doppelgängers. Not many animals in the swamp were the size of one human, let alone two.

She patted him between his eye bumps. "You did good."

She hadn't done badly herself with three doppelgängers

down and no human casualties. Out in the swamp, she could give herself the rare pat on the back. Her self-congratulations didn't last long. Even though she had dispatched the demon at Riley's on her own, he had found his way to town, and there were four more to contend with.

"If I were calling the shots, what would I do with my remaining four soldiers? My enemy sent one, then two." Having a computer projection of her real's brain created a superhuman skill set in Sere that Jennifer Cranston would never master—most notably, an ability to understand mathematical concepts. "Exponential escalation—doubling the attack force with each conflict. He'll go all in with his last four combat drones."

With the shotgun between her knees looking like a crumpled straw some child had chewed, she was down one of her most potent weapons. Beheading doppelgängers provided a much-needed release for her combat lust, but those hand-to-hand altercations worked better one-on-one. Taking on four at once—even if they lacked Sere's fighting skills—would create too many variables.

"Guess I'll be slinking back to Joe's cabin with my tail between my legs. I hate leaving the swamp unattended. Hopefully I'll have better luck talking to the hunters out here on the water, where they work, than dealing with their drunk asses at Riley's."

Lefty lowered his head below the water, sending a wave over his back that drenched Sere's legs. She jumped to her feet and grabbed her shotgun before it could float off Lefty's back. "Hey, now. That was uncalled for. I know you'll remain on guard duty out here. You're still my first line of defense, but I need people to do their part as well. After all, these demons aren't coming to the land of the living to collect alligator hides. Those who are in the most danger should at least take on the responsibility of identifying the enemy."

5

*S*ere stood on the back of her giant alligator as he swam out of the cypress grove and back into the hunting grounds. The evening sun was just touching the horizon over the bayou, casting her long shadow over the water. Her pulse raced as she guided Lefty with her feet toward the main river that connected the tracts of wetlands. "Don't worry, old friend, the gator hunters can't hurt you. Those puny bullets would just bounce right off your hide."

If one of those idiots did have the stupidity to shoot, however, and the ricochet managed to hit Sere, things would get a little dicier. Their confirmation of the thirty-foot-gator myth would bring more than enough trouble. Having a swamp witch heal from a bullet wound right before their eyes was not an option. Some magical abilities were best left unseen.

She rested her hand on the butt of her chomped-barrel shotgun. At least it still fit in her thigh holster. At the shock of seeing a mythical alligator and its supposedly armed mistress, the testosterone-fueled hunters would hopefully think twice about whipping out their weapons.

She pulled a couple of cartridges from her bullet belt and tossed them in the river behind Lefty. "You're more than enough gator for anyone, but a little backup couldn't hurt. Plus, those river lizards could use a little courage. Seeing you and me deal with their murderers just might give us some reptilian support in our quest to contain hell."

Lefty continued his gentle rocking through the water, seemingly oblivious to the dozen gators that had fallen in line behind him. As they rounded a bend, Sere saw the first indication that they were getting close to their prey. A dead chicken dangled from a rope tied to a sapling.

"Take me over there. I can't afford to have one of our friends succumb to his hunger and end up thrashing for his life. The gator hunters need to know I'm in control—not guiding their catch straight to them."

Lefty drifted slowly up to the hunk of meat, which looked like a small dog treat compared to his massive body. Sere pulled out her knife and cut the rope, then she removed the massive hook and tossed the morsel behind Lefty. The gators that followed him fought over the meal like a bunch of angry seagulls. "I suppose it's reptilian nature not to share."

She needed to make as big an impact on the men as possible. Running across a lone hunter and relying on him to spread the word wasn't going to be enough to secure the help she needed. She stepped up to Lefty's massive shoulders and stood tall, hoping to look like a captain piloting her ship. "We'll head straight toward the dock. Right now the rivermen are probably making the final checks of their lures. If we beat them back to the dock, not only will we command all of their attention, but we'll also have them by the short hairs as they'll be in a hurry to offload before sunset."

Lefty followed the directions of her feet as if her words didn't matter. She could hear the outboard motors from across the open grasslands. No ripples disturbed the water ahead of her, however. "Since this is the main tributary back to town, they probably put off checking these traps until last. They're about to be wildly disappointed."

Each line they came to became one more hunk of chicken for her gator navy or one more freed alligator recruit who'd bitten at the wrong piece of meat. Lefty rounded the final bend leading to the dock. Though the area along the river was still empty, the open-sided processing warehouse was filling with laborers and buyers preparing to weigh and measure the day's catch.

"I want them to get a good look at you. Think you can climb up on the wharf?"

Lefty put his massive clawed foot on the back of the floating wood pier and rocked it hard to the side like a canoe being boarded from the water. When he managed to get his second front leg up on the structure, the far end lifted six feet off the river. The commotion emptied the warehouse as men came running to investigate.

Sere used Lefty's scutes as footholds to maintain her standing position on his back as he climbed onto the rickety structure. The boards creaked and snapped under his massive frame. When he had finally hauled his body onto the wharf, it looked like a child's air mattress in a pool that some fat uncle had commandeered. Only the pilings were still above the water line. The other alligators milled around him, filling up the small bay.

Men stood dumbstruck at the water's edge. Sere kept her hand on the butt of her useless shotgun. "Everyone, just take it easy. We're going to hang out here until all the hunters return from their day on the river. I don't want to have to explain myself twice."

A man pushed his way through the crowd. With his girth, he had to be the lead buyer. "Lady, I'll give you a king's ransom for that beast."

She gripped the gun so hard the end of the holster pointed up from her leg like a teenage boy's erection. "One more comment like that, and my friend here might get the wrong idea. He has quite the appetite, so we wouldn't want things to turn ugly."

The fat man backed away from the water's edge. "I didn't mean any disrespect, but that is quite the animal, as are the pack you've brought with him. I'll bet not one of them is less than twelve feet in length. What are you, some sort of swamp witch?"

"I was raised by one, but I'm much more than that now."

She turned back to the water as the first sounds of outboard motors echoed in from the trees. *Finally.* As the tired men caught sight of the estuary filled with alligators they started pulling out their rifles.

"First one of you to pull a trigger is going to be gator food," she yelled.

"Goddamn you, scrawny-ass bitch!" Cody's voice cut through the noise of the motors.

The smell of dead gator that emanated from each of the johnboats filled the air like swamp gas. Though Lefty remained on the dock, sunning himself in the last rays of daylight, the other gators grew restless to investigate the scents of their dead companions. The water started boiling from the action of their tails, mirroring the energy Sere sensed from the hunters. *Things are about to get out of hand.*

"I'm not here to start a war between humans and reptiles. Something far more dangerous is headed in from the deep swamp, and I'll need all of your help to stop the demons before they make it to shore and raise holy hell."

The johnboats drifted out of their dense pack—each bow aimed at a different circling gator. From her perch on top of Lefty, Sere saw the gleam of rifle barrels secretly being made ready for the slaughter. "If any of you make one more move against these gators, you'll find your boats snapped in half."

In spite of Sere's show of feminine power and animal strength, the men's attentions were fixed on the prize catches floating so close to their processing facility. She nudged Lefty in the side. "Time to get to work, my friend. Seems like these assholes aren't going to listen without a demonstration of superiority."

The giant creature arched his body to the side, snapping the pier pilings like matchsticks. His loud splash sent a wave of water across the estuary, forcing the gator navy away from the boats with their men and weapons. Lefty used his fifteen-foot tail to flip around and dart toward the lead bow.

Whether out of fear, greed, or foolishness, the hunter rose up out of his crouched position and fired his rifle. The bullet harmlessly bounced off Lefty's snout.

"Well, now, that was just plain stupid," Sere said as Lefty opened his cavernous jaws. With one chomp he crushed the front of the boat into kindling.

The man fell on his butt and crab walked back to his partner at the outboard motor. As what was left of the hull filled with water, both men scampered over the back transom. Their catch of three good-sized carcasses slipped into the watery grave.

"If you're quick, you just might be able to swim to shore before Lefty's friends get any ideas about seeking revenge," Sere said to the men in the water. Lefty took aim at the next nearest boat. "Now, would any of the rest of you like to test out your peashooters?"

Cody stood, put his foot on his boat's thwart, and aimed his rifle at Sere's head. "What if I just shoot you instead?"

"Try it, asshole. But before you do, ask yourself what my snakes might think of your threat. Do you really think the swamp's creatures are going to take kindly to you hurting their mistress? You're all outnumbered by the reptiles, fish, and bugs out here, and you know it. All it would take is a little organization by these critters, and none of you would be able to set foot in the swamp ever again."

The boat floating precariously in front of Lefty's razor-sharp teeth abruptly swung to the side, which positioned it between Cody and Sere. The hunter stood and held his hands out from his sides to show that he wasn't holding a weapon. "What is it you want from us?"

"A temporary truce. You're hunters, and I'm not going to tell you not to make a living. But you're not to kill any alligator over twelve feet in length. I need these big boys to be my guardians in the deep swamp."

"What exactly do you think is out there?" he asked.

"To you, they'll look like city folk who got lost in the swamp."

"Not this bullshit again," Cody yelled from behind the lead boat. "Was that poor fat fuck you were hunting months ago some lover who dumped your bony ass? You can't still be looking for revenge. Accept that he's better off without you, and find some other poor sap to screw." He laughed, but no one else joined in.

"Monty has been dealt with, no thanks to you, but he showed the escape route for others to follow. Of course, you already know that. After all, it was you who gave his kin a ride in from hell's gate the other day."

Cody shook his head in a show of disbelief. "Girly, I've met some people out here who don't take kindly to strangers, but you take the cake. Not everyone who gets lost in the swamp is a serial killer."

Well, he didn't mention yesterday's bar brawl decapitation. That's something at least. Riley must be trying to keep the incident quiet. Either she's worried about killings affecting her business, or she knows about the demons and has further use for them.

"And I'm hoping not every alligator hunter is as ignorant an asshole as you are," Sere said. "I'm not asking you to confront every stranger you run across—quite the opposite. If one of them does survive his encounter with my reptilian friends in the deep swamp, you probably won't want to approach the mangled remains anyway. Just get word to the bikers about what you see. They'll relay the message to me."

"And what do we get in return?" The man standing in the lead boat had barely taken his eyes off Lefty since they'd arrived.

Sere couldn't see any point in hiding the truth. Either the men would be inclined to give her the benefit of the doubt now, or they would be convinced when the torn-to-shreds doppelgängers came after them like a zombie horde leading the apocalypse. She chose her words carefully. "If I can't stop this invasion, your swamp is about to become the hellmouth. Right now, only humanlike creatures have figured out how to cross over, but once they start coming through in large numbers, you can bet other monsters will follow. If you think Lefty is impressive, wait until you meet his parents."

The man nodded toward Lefty's massive snout. "If they're anything like that pet of yours, I say let them through."

Just like a man, she thought. He'd condemn the living to hell just to make a killing. "Even if you had a rifle big enough," she said, "these creatures can't be killed by your measly bullets. All you would do is piss them off."

"I'll take my chances. Now, if you don't have anything else to offer other than empty threats, would you mind letting us deliver our catch? It's getting late, and we've all still got to make our weigh-ins."

"FUCKING IDIOT ASSHOLES." Sere stood on the shore and continued her line of mumbling expletives. Though there was little she could do, she chose to stay until Lefty had escorted his living brethren out of harm's way. Without the prospect of gathering the last-minute hides, the gator hunters hardly gave her a second glance. They unloaded their boats on the makeshift gangway they'd set up to replace the dock.

She didn't really care that the men probably wouldn't survive the week. They'd been warned. The best she could hope for was that word of their slaughter would filter back to the bikers and, through them, to Bart.

She walked away from the facility, mumbling, "The loas of the dead will have their hands full processing so many spirits. That should buy me a little time before I have to face those soul-stealing bastards. At least the alligators are on my side. If they can manage the killings before the doppelfuckers, the loas won't suspect anything out of the ordinary."

How the loas had reacted to Monty's killings, however, was still a mystery. Either those immortal pricks were dumber than she thought and didn't realize the killings hadn't happened in the normal way, or she had friends intervening somewhere. As for the swamp creatures, she feared her words hadn't meant a damn thing. The doppelgängers weren't after them. Lefty, however, would command the respect of even the most hardened of animals. They would follow him to the edge of hell—though if the remaining batch of doppelgängers went on a killing spree, relying on the alligators to stop all of hell's new recruits seemed like a long shot.

She walked into town, dejected. None of her allies were rock-solid. The bikers might keep their eyes open for something unusual, but they were only trying to curry favor with Bart. Any sighting from the sloshed slugs would be unreliable. The offer of free drinks had a way of making barflies see things that weren't there.

She'd fared even worse with the gator hunters. If anything, those assholes might give a demon a ride into town if they stumbled across one, as Cody had. Since Bart was offering a free drink for information, Riley might forgive an entire bar tab for the delivery of another demonic customer just to compete.

The alligators were her best bet, but even they were motivated more by food than fear. The paranormal buckshot that she'd used as her calling card only went so far. If she did manage to slow down the four demons, that would only leave the gators with no new doppelgängers from hell to eat. She couldn't rely on them hanging around the interdimensional gate forever. Lefty was the only creature she could really count on out here—and maybe Bart.

She snuck back into Larry's machine shop, not that anyone seemed to be paying any attention. By the time the gator hunters had finished retelling the story over their dinners she'd be the laughingstock of the town. Guys who were overly concerned about their masculinity couldn't help but put down a woman who'd shown some backbone. They would probably belittle her alligator contingent like guys bragging about their own dick sizes. Their catches would certainly sound far more impressive than the swamp lizards she'd tricked into swimming along with her. In any case, she had more important issues to deal with than hunter stories.

"Fuck 'em all." Sere pulled out her battered shotgun to inspect the damage. Lefty had crushed the barrels but good. "Damn it. I hate having to ask Joe for another favor." She looked around the machine shop, once again missing the master mechanic who'd been so nice to her. "I'll bet you'd have this thing fixed up in time for one of Kelly's dessert pies."

Her obligation to the people Monty had ruined would be nothing compared to the carnage caused by the demons that would follow. To keep the memories fresh, she counted out the individuals on her fingers. "First, there's Larry. The sweet man was just trying to help. If I hadn't been in such a hurry to get my motorcycle back, I might have noticed I was being followed. Then, Kelly suffered the same fate for the same reason. I don't even know the names of the rest of the people Monty killed while perfecting his murderous habit, only that a total of seven were reported on by the news. I guess that's another thing for my to-do list—I need to get a copy of that news report or go to the cops for the files. Yeah, that should be easy, since I'm their number-one suspect and any request could put me behind bars."

But her debt didn't end with those who'd lost their lives. She continued with her self-flagellating list. "Montgomery Fisher, CPA, I haven't forgotten you. I swore I'd get that demon out of you, and I will." She lifted another finger next to the one representing Monty's real. "Thomas is completely my fault. I can't even blame some doppelgänger for his troubles. Once I figure out how to save Mr. Fisher, I'll be headed your way." She stared at her fingers. She was responsible for nine souls, eight of which were just the result of one demon finding his way out of hell.

The two canebrake rattlesnakes slithered against her feet. "I do still have you two. Guess I'm just better at fighting than persuading."

She pulled her leather riding pants, halter top, and boots from her saddlebags. There was no other option than to leave the protection of the swamp in Lefty's capable jaws. If the demons did make it by him, the best she could do was establish a barrier between the Northshore and New Orleans.

Without the shotgun, the holster around her leg was like the phantom pain of a missing limb. She lifted the mangled hunk of metal from Larry's workbench. Though having it strapped to her leg would give her a sense of balance, giving in to the temptation to pull it out in a fight would leave her unarmed.

She snapped open the barrels and pulled out the shells. "No point in wasting ammunition." The single-barrel gun that she usually kept in her bedroll for emergencies wouldn't afford her much protection in a fight, but it would at least buy her some time to escape. She pulled it out from under the headlight and dropped it into the oversized holster. It rattled loosely in the leather pocket.

Finally, she lifted the snakes from the floor and returned

them to her saddlebags. "I suppose this is the best I can expect until I reach Joe."

Night had fallen by the time she wheeled her Triton out of the mechanic's garage. No one seemed to pay much attention to her as she fired up the old motor. She felt like an unwanted stray dog that was leaving town.

Before taking a left onto the dark highway that wound around the swamp, she looked back at the sleepy little hamlet. "Hell is coming, and you fools don't even care."

6

*E*ven with the Triton's motor working like a white-noise machine on the long ride down to Joe's cabin, Sere was pissed. "What's the point in trying to protect people who never listen?"

Sure, she had a personal motive in sending the demons back to hell. She wasn't so delusional as to think her actions were in any way altruistic. After all, the only people she'd met in life who had been truly nice to her had been killed. But maintaining the balance between the living, the dead, and the damned also wasn't purely for her own protection. People had a right to be safe from beings from other dimensions. "That may be the only thing I have in common with these people. They shouldn't be killed by demons, and I shouldn't have my soul stolen by the loas of the dead."

She'd been back among the living for months, and so far, the loas hadn't caught on to her deception. "I'm just being paranoid. So long as the loas can't connect me to the death of a living human being, there's no reason for them to come looking for me. With seven billion souls wandering the earth, they can't keep tabs on everyone."

She was special, though—the only soul stolen from Guinee—and the devil himself had made her that way. That wasn't the type of action the loas could let stand. The memory of being a little girl standing on the river's levee with Sanguine's protective wings shielding her from the storm still haunted Sere.

"What just happened?" she'd asked. As a child looking up at the magical angel, Sere couldn't understand why the others hadn't simply turned her back over to the lords of the afterlife.

"Hell has lost its devil." A crystal-clear tear fell from Sanguine's magical eye.

"I don't even know what that means," Sere said.

"In life, your father's actions earned him the title of devil. To avoid death, he deceived the loas of the dead and ended up joining them as their most powerful baron. Even then, he wasn't satisfied, and no one is hated more than a person who betrays his companions. With his new immortality and power, Baron Malveaux rejoined the living in an attempt to rule over that dimension as well. If it hadn't been for my grandmother spending her life building this place, Kendell stumbling across the curse that would be his undoing, and more voodoo magic than you can imagine, he might have succeeded."

Sere never was a fan of long-winded explanations. "What does that have to do with me?" she'd asked.

The angel had caressed Sere's gossamer red hair. "You are the love that saved him."

Took his place, more like, Sere thought as she raced down the highway. Kendell and Myles secretly dumping her father's black soul into the *deep waters*—the source of all humanity—had ended him as a threat. The loas, however, demanded a reckoning. Leaving Sere in hell had balanced the equation. Sere had expressed that idea to her guardian angel on several occasions.

"That's not what happened," Sanguine would reply. "Your father sacrificed his existence so you could have a life. You were so young when you died."

Sere squeezed the handgrips of her motorcycle. *You all kept saying that I died, like I wasn't responsible for what happened. I killed myself, even if it was the curse that finished me off.* But the fact that she'd put herself in Guinee didn't mean she had any desire to return there. As a little girl, she'd felt helpless against the evils of her father. Now that she'd grown and escaped to the life those around her believed she should have, she might be the only one who could save humanity from her father's hell.

So long as the loas believed the evil baron's soul was still being held prisoner by Sanguine and Kendell, a détente between the three dimensions was maintained. But if they ever figured out that it was the baron, and not Sere, who had been poured back into the *deep waters*, they would reopen the case. And because she was no longer in hell, they'd find that voodoo box empty. Too many people had put too much on the line for her to act recklessly with the living souls she ran across. Any unexplained death could lead to her unmasking. Once discovered, there would be no one capable of defending the living from hell's fury.

She twisted the throttle as far as it would go. Untangling the knot of souls was for other, smarter people. She'd been trained to take action.

But just like these dumb rural fucks, I've been refusing the help that's most obvious. Looks like I owe Kendell and Myles an apology next time I'm in New Orleans.

Though she didn't want to face the inevitability of leaving her adopted swamp home, she *was* headed south. Once she was done with Joe, there weren't a lot of options of where to make her stand outside of the big city. But whatever her history and her future, the fact remained: she owed a debt to the living.

SERE SHUT down her motorcycle a half mile from Joe's cabin. The man had an unnerving ability to wake up at the slightest unexpected rustling of the trees. At two in the morning, she couldn't imagine a better time to conduct a sneak attack on her mentor.

As was frequently the case in the bayou, not a single leaf stirred in the night air. She watched the shadows cast by the moonlight for any indication of movement. A lone pine bough lazily waved from an owl taking flight.

I suppose it wouldn't be any fun if creeping up on him was easy. She carefully leaned back against the motorcycle seat to strip off her shotgun holster, leather jacket, and alligator boots. Though she didn't need the protection of her Ranger knife, Joe would consider her attack only half-successful if she showed up without it. The cold steel chilled her back as she slid the blade under the catch of her halter top.

Even at that distance from his cabin, she eased off the motorcycle to prevent the springs from making any sound. She stared at the dark structure nestled far off in the trees. *There's no point in searching for a light. If he does hear me, it's not like he's going to announce that fact. The cat doesn't yell "I see you" to the mouse. If he spots me, he'll conduct a counterattack. And knowing Joe, I'll never see it coming. I need those eyes in the back of my head that he keeps talking about.*

The shadows made a random lace pattern along the path. *If he's asleep, the dirt road will make an easier approach— fewer twigs and rocks that might give me away. If he's awake, however, he'll certainly notice me moving in the moonlight.*

She edged into the small grass field beside the motorcycle. Dew had formed on the tender blades from the ever-present humidity, wetting her bare feet. *Damp vegetation makes less noise but leaves a clearer track.* She bent down to read the glen. The evenly spaced claw prints of a possum trailed along the road while a curving line indicated that a large snake hadn't been far behind, sneaking through the grass.

Sere ran the blades between her fingertips. *No new droplets. They must have passed just before I pulled up.*

She chose the snake's path, which wound along the edge of the trees. With her toes, she felt the narrow line of flattened vegetation. The temptation to hurry along the established route conflicted with her desire to remain as invisible as possible. *I need to be in position in case those two animals have it out. They'd make a perfect distraction.*

The snake continued hunting its prey along the side of the road, just far enough in the shadows that Sere felt confident she hadn't been seen. When her toes encountered the mat of pine needles that surrounded Joe's cabin, she turned toward the river and away from the snake's pursuit. She crouched low behind a tree trunk and checked her analog watch. *2:45 a.m. Fifteen minutes. Not bad.*

The cabin remained dark and quiet. If Joe had woken up, he wasn't making any indication. She listened hard, hoping to catch any sound at all. *He probably taught himself how not to snore.*

As a child, waiting had always been the hardest part of her sneak attacks. She well remembered the week Joe had assigned her to shadow a black panther in order to learn the art of savoring the pursuit. The great cat acted like she had all the time in the world while on the prowl. Only at the moment of the kill did the huntress release her full strength and speed.

A barely heard rustling on the far side of the cabin indicated the snake had made its move. The battle wouldn't last long and would undoubtedly attract Joe's attention. On the rocks nestled among the potentially noisy needles, Sere danced like a ninja ballerina, twirling on her toes. She sprinted up to the wood deck behind the cabin just as the possum let out its death cry.

Sere's heart was pounding hard. She'd never before made it onto Joe's deck unobserved—though just because he hadn't hit the floodlights didn't mean he wasn't playing with her. She pulled the knife from her back and slid it between the door and the frame. *Only one lock.* Based on the complexity that he put into securing his hidden caches, she wasn't sure if she should have expected more or if he simply relied on his skills over mechanical tricks. The hasp made a soft click as she pressed the knife into the gap. She slid the glass door open just wide enough to squeeze through.

The razor-sharp edge of an assassin's knife sliced just deep enough into the base of Sere's throat that she stood stone-still.

"Not bad." Joe eased off on the pressure of the blade against her skin.

Fuck. "What tipped you off?"

He flipped on the lights before finally taking the knife away from her neck. "It was the snake attack. The little slithery bastards never strike this close to the cabin. Usually, they wait until they're at the water's edge, where they feel more at ease. I had to assume that either the possum suspected he was being followed, or the snake thought she had competition."

Damn it! "So you were just playing with me by letting me make it into the cabin this time?" She turned to face him. He was still wearing only his boxer shorts.

"The snake put me on edge. I didn't know for sure that I was being played until I heard the lock pop open. You're getting quite good with those gymnast moves, Sere." Joe wasn't one for false compliments. Using her name was all the praise she needed or was likely to receive. "What brings you out here at this hour?"

"Lefty munched my shotgun." She felt like a stupid

schoolgirl telling her teacher that her dog had eaten her homework.

"Is his aim any better than yours?" There was the snarky Joe she knew and loved.

"Barely." Giving Joe as much information as possible often resulted in him coming up with unexpected strategies, so she laid out all latest developments. "I've all but been run out of the parish. Bart is still on my side, but he's too lazy to get out from behind his bar. Lefty is doing what he can to protect hell's gate. Other than those two, I've kind of made a mess of things. Riley has sworn to shoot me on sight. Her regulars are more apt to buy a demon a drink than try to kill it. And the bikers will only help enough to get them their next free beer. Basically, I'm persona non grata up there."

"So what's your plan?" Joe asked. "You just going to ride up and down the highway shouting 'The demons are coming' to every house you pass, Paulette Revere?"

Does he take anything seriously? "Even I know rumors spread fast up there. By tomorrow morning, I'll be the laughingstock of the Northshore. But if I don't figure out a way to stop the remaining four doppelgängers from going on killing sprees, demons will start coming out of the swamp like termites swarming on a humid summer night."

Joe pulled out a section of welded tubing, marked off the length with a piece of chalk, and started the old-fashioned nickel-plated grinder.

I've seen this before. He thinks best when his hands are busy. She sat quietly on the work stool like a child watching her father putting together a prized toy.

He didn't speak until he had the gun barrels filed down and ready for the stock. "So you're headed back to New Orleans?"

"I don't see much choice. Without me stopping them up north, the doppelgängers will be headed for their reals in the city. If I can get eyes on the potential victims, hopefully we can stop the demons before it's too late."

His stare reminded her of how she analyzed a room: cold, calculating, and searching for assets and liabilities. "Bullshit. You plan on making yourself the target. Protecting other people would involve enlisting help, and you want to go this alone."

Damn you, Joe. Why can't I ever keep anything secret from you?

"I'm not going into hiding," she said. "Trying to disguise my appearance only handicapped me against Monty. If I'm right about my opponent's thinking, the four will make a concerted attack on me. They'll want me out of the way before they go on their killing sprees. Once they create enough dead bodies, they'll go after their reals and take over their lives. At least, that's what I'd promise them if I were leading the attack—their version of Nirvana. I'm guessing that what happened to Monty before I decapitated him wouldn't be common knowledge in hell."

"I see. So you'll just stand out in the middle of the freeway, aiming your blaster at every car that passes?" He held up the four-barrel length of pipe. "Sure you don't want me to make up a second one of these so you'll have two monster-shooting scatterguns?"

"Stop making fun of me." As a young girl living in

antebellum New Orleans, Sere hadn't been able to control her rage when she was teased. Some things never changed. "I have a few days at least before these assgängers find their way to the big city. I'll blend in without hiding and round up what help I can. By the time they show up, I'll be ready."

Joe loaded a couple of cartridges in the barrels and snapped the gun closed. "I'll do what I can to spot the demons and get word to you. Use your time wisely. There's plenty of help down there. All you need to do is ask."

7

*N*ew Orleans loomed over Lake Pontchartrain in the predawn light like a spectral city of the dead. Even in the living dimension, the towers that dominated the skyline didn't show much life until midmorning. Sere discreetly peered in the car windows at the people who shared the road with her at four in the morning. Each vehicle was filled with partiers up too late or low-level employees up too early. Neither set of commuters looked overly enthusiastic. She swung her Triton past the dozing drivers like an irritated emergency worker forcing a truck through lanes of disoriented tourists.

She had people she could call on in New Orleans who would be happy to help. They needed to be informed of the dangers. But contacting any of them would put her on the path to having other people think they were in charge of the situation.

Why does everyone think they understand hell better than I do? The answer wasn't really all that complicated. Professor Yates, with his lab full of equipment, was responsible for projecting the human images into hell that resulted in the doppelgänger population. Kendell had lent her spirit as part of the dimensional prison that had incarcerated Sere's father. On and on the list went, each person claiming to have some unique perspective that made him or her the perfect candidate for directing the paranormal defenses against hell's demons.

The best defense is a good offense. The concept was far from new, but Joe had made it the cornerstone of his teachings. Ultimately, Sere would contact the people who had been as much her family as her educators, but while she was still a step ahead of the demons, she wanted to utilize that advantage. Talking with Kendell and her crew invariably took so long that Sere would lose her strongest advantage and end up playing catch-up.

She took an unassuming exit off the freeway before it snaked into the heart of the city. Though those she trusted had their tentacles in hell, she needed someone with a more direct connection to the demons—someone the evil genius behind the demons' escape wouldn't suspect. She kept the Triton's RPMs as low as possible to avoid unnecessarily bothering the residents of the stately houses. Like a long-lost daughter sneaking back home, she felt both out of place on her café racer and at ease with the wealth and luxury that emanated from the mansions. A feeling of understated opulence surrounded her like the smell of night jasmine— all-encompassing but coming from an unidentifiable source.

She coasted the motorcycle up alongside the black Jeep Cherokee on the short driveway. The house was dark with the exception of the well-lit kitchen. A man was fumbling around, making coffee, oblivious to Sere's approach.

This isn't an attack. I don't need to be so damn covert all of the time. She stepped out of the shadows behind the Jeep. As she walked along the brick entrance, the man looked up from his morning routine and smiled at her. *At least you're mostly happy to see me.*

He greeted her at the door before she had a chance to ring the bell and wake the rest of the house. "I hope you have good news for me."

"I wish that was why I came. I'm still working on removing the demon from inside you, but that's not why I'm here. I need your help. Your doppelgänger has inspired followers."

Montgomery Fisher—CPA, husband, father, and demonically possessed—stood aside to let Sere in. "Let me get you a cup of coffee. How do you take it?"

"Black..." *Like my soul,* she thought. *Though maybe sometimes it takes darkness to combat evil... I really need to work on self-acceptance. It's just a cup of coffee, not an existential crisis.*

He led the way to the kitchen and pulled a purple-and-gold LSU cup off the shelf. The brew was so strong it looked black as ink as it flowed from the glass pot into the ceramic mug. "We can talk out in the courtyard. With this summer heat, early mornings are about the only real time I get outdoors."

Sere followed him out the kitchen side door to the well-maintained garden behind the house. She wasn't sure if he was stalling or simply didn't want to contaminate his domestic bliss with a conversation about his possessed state of being. Outdoors, with wild animals lurking in the shadows, was a fitting location for a man fighting an internal battle.

"You're handling your condition better than I'd expected."

He sat on the garden bench swing and looked at the moon that was just fading into the early dawn. "Some days are better than others. At least I have a focus for the negative emotions. Defining where they come from helps me remain in control."

Fuck. I'm about to make your life so much worse. "Without the body that was powered from hell, Monty has been cut off from that dimension's energy."

The kindly accountant took a deep swallow of his coffee. "Now that others are here, do you expect him to reach out to them?"

"I don't know what to expect. When Monty was a separate being, he had the power to draw on your energy. Once I decapitated him and his energy fused with yours, I hoped the only thing left for you to deal with would be his desires. There is a threat, however, that with hell coming to the living, that evil side of you might get fed hell's energy from the other doppelgängers. Think of it as being like a diver whose oxygen had run out. Another diver could give him a burst of air from his own tank."

Mr. Fisher gently rocked the swing with his feet. "So

you're here like some witch doctor making a house call to check on her patient?"

I'll bet you've used this swing a thousand times to calm your daughters from some fear or hurt, she thought. "I'm here because I need your help. If the doppelgängers do make it out of the swamp and find transportation down to New Orleans, you'll be the first to notice their presence."

"I see. I'll be like your early-warning detection system." He looked downcast.

"I know that's not what you were hoping I'd say. You can tell me to fuck off. I wouldn't blame you. I've already put you through way more than any human being has a right to do to another."

He stared up at the predawn sky as if searching for an answer. "There are times when a person drops the documents that sum up their financial life on my desk, and they give me this sheepish look. It's not embarrassment or even fear—more like pleading for a connection in their time of trouble." He turned to her. "You see, what I do isn't simply a matter of untangling a person's money troubles. I'm putting my name and reputation next to theirs. We face the enemy—or rather, the government, which my clients often see as the same thing—together."

"So am I the client or the professional?"

He leaned back into the wooden swing and sipped his coffee. "I suppose a little of both, as am I. We're stronger and better able to face hell together. I'd be happy to throw my lot in with you."

"Partners, then?"

He looked down and smiled. "The young, attractive,

badass, motorcycle-riding superhero and her middle-aged, slightly portly, bookish sidekick? Even my family would laugh at that image."

She put her hand on his. "Mr. Fisher, you're an educated businessman who has fought his personal demons and has the inner strength to face the unknown with determination and a sense of humor. I'll take that guy as a partner anytime."

Even in the dim light she could see the blush tinge his cheeks. "If I'm going to be working with you, we need to find a less formal address than *mister*. How about just calling me Fisher? I haven't gone by my last name since high school, but it reminds me of being on the lacrosse team. Seems fitting to me."

"Teammates then. Just don't go calling me Badass Demon Huntress—at least not in public."

Though Sere had hoped to secure Fisher's help, she hadn't expected him to lend her one of his offices as her base of operations. She set her saddlebags on a metal desk that she guessed hadn't been used in a decade, based on the amount of dust that drifted into the air. The single window was so caked with grime that even without a window covering, privacy wasn't an issue.

"It's not much," he said. "I used to bring in an associate to help with the tax-season load, but lately, I haven't found anyone I trust."

"It's perfect."

"What kind of hellholes have you worked in? Wait. Don't answer that."

She favored him with a half laugh at his lame joke. "I need to stay under the radar. If I go asking any of the people I know for help, their actions could too easily be picked up by whatever force is behind these escapes from hell. I don't need a second-line parade announcing my return to the big city. Working out of a CPA's broom closet is everything I could hope for."

"Well, the office is yours for as long as you like. If you're interested in something to do between demon outbreaks, I can put you on the payroll. There are always clients who need their stories investigated before I trust putting my reputation on the line. Some of those research projects can get a little dicey. People become defensive when I express my doubt regarding their financial records. Having someone who knows how to protect herself and doesn't mind digging into the seedier side of New Orleans could be a great help. Think it over. If you need anything, just push down on the big bar to talk to Linda. I'm afraid the intercom system is straight out of the 1970s."

Sere gingerly tapped on the yellowed plastic button. "Communications devices don't work so well around me. It has something to do with wireless systems and the strange energy I emit."

"What do you want, dear?" Linda's voice crinkled out of the old speaker.

Sere pulled her hand away as if a demon had escaped from the box. "Jesus, that thing works?"

Fisher lifted the dried, cracked telephone line from the back of the intercom. "Like I told you—vintage electronics."

Interesting. Direct-wired communication isn't affected by my energy.

"I'll try not to be in your way," she said. "Mostly, I just need a place to stash my gear. Is there a way to lock the office?"

The CPA jiggled the antique door handle. "Even if there was, one good shake of this old door, and the hasp would come out of the latch. I have complete trust in Linda."

Sere pulled her bullet belt from her saddlebag. One of the snakes came along for the ride. She laid the two on the desk. "So long as she doesn't get freaked out by seeing things other than financial records."

He blocked the entrance with his body and discreetly shut the door. "I see your point. I'll have building maintenance rig something by lunch." He took a seat opposite her in the guest chair, looking entirely too excited. "So what's our first superhero challenge?"

Shit. Now I need to give him something to keep him busy so he doesn't go running around the city doing something stupid.

"Well," she said, "I've got Professor Yates working on identifying the real people who mirror the seven original escapees, but since I haven't heard anything from him, I'm guessing he hasn't found anything. You could go check on his progress."

The CPA grimaced. "Errand boy? That's not what I had in mind."

She shrugged. "Sorry. I guess I'm not very good at delegating tasks. I only figured out Monty was after you because the professor's equipment detected him sneaking out of hell. This new batch of demons appears to have learned from that first mistake."

Fisher leaned back in the metal-and-cloth chair, drumming on the armrest with his fingers as if working an old-fashioned adding machine. "From Monty's memories, one of his first big issues was getting down to New Orleans. Without money, travel can be a real challenge. If these new demons have learned from his experiences, one of their first chores will be laying their hands on some cash."

She could tell he was going somewhere, but the path was as squirrelly as a deer trail through tall grass. "What are you thinking?"

"They're doppelgängers, which means they could easily imitate the real people they're based on, right?"

She nodded. "Obviously."

"So why not just walk into a bank and say 'I lost my wallet'? Between the doppelgänger's knowledge of their real's bank passwords, identical fingerprints, and photo IDs that would be on file, they could take out as much cash as they wanted."

Sere began to get a glimpse of where the money expert was headed. "Their reals would see the activity and think their accounts had been hacked."

"Exactly." Fisher took out a pad from his breast pocket and began furiously making notes. "With my bank contacts, that's something I can trace. If you're right about the remaining four doppelgängers exiting the swamp in the same general area, there should be a handful of accounts all being raided from somewhere on the Northshore." He got up like a cub reporter excited to follow a lead. "I'll get right on this. With any luck, I should have some clues by the end of the day."

Sere found his inquisitive mind encouraging. "There's one other person you might look out for. I only know him as Thomas. In hell, his doppelgänger was Professor Yates's assistant. Because he was something of a doppelgänger hybrid, when he died, his energy transferred to his real." Sere couldn't bring herself to tell Fisher about how she'd also beheaded that demon. "The real Thomas has already threatened to kill me once. It'd be useful to keep tabs on the little prick. I suspect he still has a contact in hell."

"You think he's the one behind these escapes?"

"I don't know where he fits in, only that he didn't have much trouble finding me. Anyone with that level of insider information makes me nervous."

Fisher made some more notes on his pad. "Tell me what you remember. I've been able to reconstruct a person's financial history with surprisingly inane details."

Sere couldn't imagine how her short captivity could be used to track down the bastard, but anything that kept Fisher busy would amount to time she didn't have to worry about him.

---

*a*fter an hour in the small room, Sere was about to crawl out of her skin. The nondescript accountant's offices on a quiet back alleyway of the Quarter made for a handy place for her to stash her gear, but boxes weren't good places to think. *Every superhero needs their privacy: Batman his cave, Superman his phone booth, and Sere Mal-Laurette—demon hunter and immortal doppelgänger—her CPA's broom closet.* The thought nearly made her laugh.

She checked her bullet belt to be sure she'd replaced the shells she'd used in the swamp. The new shotgun Joe had worked up fit comfortably in the holster against her thigh. "I don't care how I look. This is New Orleans." She headed out of her office and poked her nose into Fisher's doorway. "I'm heading out to do a little reconnaissance. Anything worth reporting on the paper trial—or anything else?" On the one hand, she hoped the kindly gentleman wasn't being pestered from the beyond, but on the other, she needed something to do while she still held the advantage.

He shrugged. "It'll take a few hours for my leads to pan out. As for the other thing, I'm afraid I'm feeling fine. I don't know what else to tell ya."

She gave him a reassuring smile. "I expect we have a day or two at least before things get interesting, but if you start getting headaches, don't rely simply on aspirin."

He shivered, probably not from the tepid air coming out of the rackety air-conditioning system. "I remember the sensation. Convulsing on the floor isn't something I'm apt to forget. If those *unwelcome clients* show up, I'll know." *Unwelcome* was as big an insult as Fisher would hurl at someone. He was no doubt watching his language for Linda's sake. "I should be back before you close up for the day. While I'm out, I'll try to come up with a communication network so you can reach me if something changes. And until they get the office lock fixed, it might be a good idea if no one messed with my saddlebags." She wiggled her forearm and wrist while making biting gestures with her hand.

Fisher's tightly pursed lips and tilted-head nod indicated that he was well aware of the snakes in the next room.

As Sere passed Linda's desk, the old receptionist didn't even look up from her dictation. "Heading out, dear?"

Yes, Mom. "Just going to check out the city." Sere looked over her shoulder at Fisher's office. "You might keep an eye on him today."

"That's my job." The woman finally looked up at Sere.

Her crystal-blue eyes were more penetrating than Sere remembered. "Be careful out there."

Carrying a loaded shotgun in public, and in a big city, seemed like a way of inviting trouble. But then, when it came to Sere, trouble never waited for an invitation. She walked the streets of the Quarter like a new sheriff getting a feel for her jurisdiction, and she tried to figure out what to do. She did need a way to communicate without modern technology and a way to keep an eye on the doppelgängers' reals—once Fisher or Professor Yates identified them.

"Damn, girl, that's some authentic-looking steampunk right there." The homeless dude who lay on a flattened piece of cardboard crammed into a doorway struggled to sit up. The peeling paint, rusted lock, and boarded-up windows of the building behind him made it clear that the place was deserted. He wasn't in danger of being kicked off the stoop anytime soon.

"We all have our part to play."

He leaned forward and spread his arms so she could get a look at his ratty coat, torn jeans, and beat-up army boots. The outfit must have been too long on his body, and with too few washings, because the color of grimy dark-green coated him from head to foot like a river rock caked in algae —and smelled about as bad. "And what would you say about my role in life's production?"

She admired the fact that he hadn't immediately hit her up for money. "That you perform your character with gusto every moment you're on the stage."

He rummaged around in the pile of food wrappers that were scattered next to him. "I've got half of a fried-fish po'boy if you're hungry. Someone dropped it off on my pad while I was sleeping."

She knew he was testing her. Instead of politely declining and walking off or tossing a few dollars to ease her discomfort, she sat on the stair below the stoop. "Have any mustard to go with it?"

He looked at her with wide eyes and a missing-tooth grin. "A fellow connoisseur. Mustard makes everything taste better." He pulled out a handful of plastic packs from his jacket and tossed her one. From the faded cartoon chicken on the label and the separated yellow concoction inside, Sere suspected the joint had closed down long ago.

"I should tell you I don't have any money." She'd handed her last few dollars to Bart for that round of drinks.

The vagrant retrieved a greasy bundle of napkins from an almost equally greasy paper bag. He unwrapped the sandwich as if preparing a romantic picnic. "I figured. People with money don't stop. The more a person has in their pocket, the less friendly they are." He split the half roll and gave her the bigger section.

The sandwich smelled as if the fish was well past its prime. *Good thing I'm not susceptible to food poisoning.* "Maybe you'd better give me two of those mustard packs."

He tossed her a handful before taking a big bite of his section. She squeezed all of the packs inside the bun before taking a small nibble. The thing tasted like a catfish that had been rotting for days on the bank of the swamp and then deep-fried in alligator piss. "I may not be as hungry as I thought."

He set his piece of the sandwich on top of the paper bag

and washed down the mouthful with a swig of Jack. "If I can't offer you something to eat, what can I do for you?"

Time to lay down my cards. "I've been living on Frenchmen Street for the last few months. Every homeless person I pass gives me a knowing smile. At first I found it discomforting, like maybe your people knew something about my past that you shouldn't. One night, I caught Myles and Kendell leaving the club. From every shadowy doorway, the homeless scanned the street as if keeping an eye out for their protection. Based on your hospitality, I suspect you know who I am. I think it might be time you explained why that is."

The guy sat a little straighter and smiled knowingly, giving Sere the impression of a spy who'd just had his cover blown. "The river angel has watched after the homeless for nearly two decades. She would be pretty upset if we let anything bad happen to you."

I knew it, she thought. "Kendell has you spying on me?"

Though the woman had contacts throughout the city—and not all of them business-related—Sere hadn't realized she'd so thoroughly organized the city's homeless. *Kendell's secret army.* So that was how she and the crew had managed to escape detection after the bank explosion that closed hell off from Guinee.

"From time to time, she asks favors from my community of miscreants. The land across the river that she secured for the homeless is a debt we'll never be able to repay. We may be destitute, but thanks to her, there's always an extended family that will welcome any of us into its arms." He looked at Sere with something approaching awe. "You're important to her, and that means we will help where we can. Just don't expect us to look the other way if you step into danger."

Kendell, the magic mother hen. "Fair enough. Right now, what I need most is a way for Montgomery Fisher to get messages to me. I also need any information you can give me about strange occurrences that even you can't explain."

He picked up his sandwich like he was slipping back into character. "I'll pass the word."

SERE SNUCK into the loft above the Scratchy Dog for a quick shower to clean off the smell and feel of rotting fish. Some prejudices died hard even to someone who'd grown up in hell. She couldn't help it if she'd been born to privilege.

At least the homeless aren't trying to shoot me like certain people on the Northshore. But the harvesters from my interdimensional nightmares come from the streets, not the mansions. The professor might want to check on his projections of the homeless class into their doppelgänger doubles.

Once clean, she stood in the middle of the walk-in storage closet full of band costumes. Her riding leathers worked well for being on the hunt, but she needed something less obvious if she expected to haul her snakes and guns around in the Quarter. That homeless fellow might have been onto something. A woman in steampunk could carry whatever weapons she wanted without being noticed.

The strapless purple-and-black-paisley leather bustier, with latches that went from cleavage to crotch, fit tightly enough that fighting wouldn't be a problem. The flowing layered Victorian dress that went with it, however, was a nonstarter. *Jeez, Kendell, how did you perform in this horror show of fabric?*

Instead, Sere chose the semirespectable sheer black-striped leggings that fit easily into her alligator-skin boots. Each item of clothing took considerable tugging to get over even her modest curves. She checked the ensemble out in the full-sized mirror at the back of the closet. On its own, the outfit made her look overly available. Seeing the shotgun holstered at her leg and knife handle prominently projecting from her boot, however, anyone would think twice about bothering her. *Once I add in the snakes around my neck, this will do nicely.*

The front door beckoned, but she wasn't going to let her earlier misstep defeat her. *It's late afternoon, so no scrambling along the front roof. Too many people below who might spot me.*

She headed to the seldom-used back dormer window. The rusty iron fire escape looked so rotted that a person would be better off facing the flames than trusting her weight to the thin steps three stories up. *Perfect.* She grabbed the top of the window frame and swung around onto the metal support rail. Hand over hand, she slid down the side of the ladder until she was able to jump the remaining ten feet to the ground.

The narrow alley was littered with used condoms, red plastic cups, and vomit. She headed straight to the back and vaulted up to the wheels of metal spikes meant to dissuade intruders. Sere grabbed the sharpened rods on two of the wheels and used her momentum to rotate the old security system away from the alley and back toward the street behind the club. She did a handspring down to the brick sidewalk like a gymnast sticking her landing. *Time to get back to work. Hopefully, someone's got some information for me by now.*

SHE PUSHED OPEN the front door of Fisher's offices, feeling more at home than she'd expected after only a day's supposed employment. "Is he in?"

Linda sat huddled over her computer like someone who had nothing to do but was trying to look busy. "I'm sorry, dear. He left early."

What's that about? "Does he do that often?"

The secretary looked relieved that Sere had somehow stumbled on the right thing to ask. "Hardly ever. He said there were a handful of prospective new accounts he wanted to meet with personally."

Fuck! Tell me you didn't go after the reals on your own. "Did he happen to leave me a note?"

"I'm afraid not, dear. Unless he left it on your desk." Linda's raised eyebrows indicated that she wasn't happy about being left out of the interoffice communication loop.

Sere looked over the secretary's shoulder at the bright, shiny new door handle and lock. "I see building maintenance was here. Do you have my new key?"

"I was instructed not to enter your office." The snark in her voice made each word stand out as if it were its own sentence.

"It was for your own good."

"Of course, dear." The woman had an amazing ability to pull the sweet-old-lady cover back over her irritation like a shawl. "I'm just letting you know that I don't have a key, so wouldn't know if Mr. Fisher left you a note or not."

Sere felt the presence of her combat knife in her boot like a scratch she dared not itch. With a couple of quick thrusts, she could defeat the lock. But that might involve building maintenance making a return visit.

What do I need in there? I've got my cache above the Scratchy Dog if I need more ammunition. Adding to Linda's fear by jimmying the lock isn't worth it, but I could sure use my snakes.

Sere picked up a small pile of business cards from the display on Linda's desk. "It's no big deal. Mr. Fisher and I discussed some new business early this morning. I'm sure he's just following up. Just the same, I'll run these around to the prospects we talked about and have them give the office a call if they see him. I'll see you in the morning."

The tightness in the woman's old shoulders noticeably eased. "I'll hang around until closing in case anyone calls or there's something else you need."

Once clear of the office's front windows, Sere edged into the used bookshop next door. She smiled sweetly at the old man behind the counter as he looked up from his crossword puzzle. "Would you mind if I used your bathroom?"

He grumbled something and nodded toward the back of the store before settling in behind his paper. At one time, the shop had probably been the mirror image of the CPA's offices. The bookstore retained the original open floor plan with a single office and bathroom in the back. She pushed open the door to the bathroom, letting the squeaky hinges work as a distraction while she snuck into the office on the other side of the hallway. As she'd hoped, the window above the desk looked exactly like the one in her office. She climbed on the chair, unlatched the ancient brass catch, lifted the double-hung window, and slipped into the interior ventilation shaft that separated the two businesses. *I doubt anyone has been in this atrium in decades.*

She jammed the tip of her knife under the window to her office and cut the paint that sealed it shut. It took a little prying to get the ancient hardware to behave. Once the window had separated from the frame by a couple of inches, she hissed into the opening. Both snakes slithered out of her bags and up the wall to the window like they'd just been sprung from prison.

With the snakes draped around her shoulders like a living necklace, Sere scurried out of the bookshop and headed down the street to where she'd stashed her Triton. The possibilities of what Fisher was up to swirled around her head like a cloud of gnats. She wished she could easily swat away each one.

If he's gone after the reals, he could be trying to warn them. Professor Yates laid out the dangers of such an action when Monty was hunting Fisher. Nothing good would come from the bait knowing it was being pursued. On the other side of the spiritual coin, Monty might be directing Fisher's actions. In which case I'm really screwed. That demon could be holding onto the reals until his brethren show up to claim them. An act like that could regain him some standing in the doppelgänger community.

Sere shook her head, trying not to focus on the worst-case scenario. *I need to find those four people, and without Fisher's help, all I have left is the professor.*

A couple of blocks from the offices was the dark alley lined with the crumbling backs of businesses. The area was inhabited exclusively by the homeless and drug addicted. The indigents nodded respectfully as Sere passed their collections of meager possessions. Her motorcycle sat untouched in the middle of the block like a priceless museum artifact being heavily guarded.

As she threw her leg over the seat, she looked down at the nearest of Kendell's spies. "Keep an eye out for Mr. Fisher. He may be in trouble."

"Do you want us to notify the river angel?" The man's drunken slur didn't inspire confidence.

"Not yet. If I don't return by start of work tomorrow, then let her know." Sere started her motorcycle without waiting for a reply. The destitute contingent wasn't hers to command, but hopefully, they wouldn't call in the cavalry until Sere had an opportunity to find out which side Montgomery Fisher was playing for.

9

The old shipping offices down on the decaying wharf were just as Sere had left them—right down to the old man hunched over his computer—with the addition of fast-food bags and half-eaten meals scattered around the floor. The professor's dedication was admirable but terrifying.

"Well, at least you must have gotten out of that chair at some point."

Professor Yates looked up with bloodshot eyes. His three-day-old beard and disheveled gray hair indicated he hadn't showered since she'd left him. "Polly's been bringing me food."

"Any conclusions on my latest targets?" Sere asked.

He squeezed his eyes closed and shook his head as if trying to remember what she was talking about. "Oh, yeah." He turned his Barcalounger to the table behind him and pulled out a sheet of paper from under the pile that filled the printer's tray. "All seven names and addresses."

Sere quickly scanned the date stamp at the top of the page. "You printed this thirty-six hours ago. Why didn't you get this to me and go home for some rest?"

He turned back to his computer as if he'd left it unattended for too long. "Those seven idiots aren't the problem. It's like a software virus..." He trailed off.

"It might help if I knew what you were talking about."

Polly came out of the back bathroom, looking only slightly more rested than the professor. "You'll have to forgive him. He gets into one of these code investigations, and he loses track of everything."

Thank God—someone who doesn't talk in riddles. Sere held up the sheet of paper. "What has he found other than these identities?"

Polly directed Sere outside, where they could talk without disturbing the mad scientist. "Hell's dimension is much worse than we remember. Something is affecting it beyond our projections."

Duh. "I could have told you that. My dreams are filled with harvesters, monstrous creatures based on real animals, and doppelgängers suffering all manner of tortures. I don't remember it being that bad as a child. I just figured without my father as the devil in charge, the realm had resorted to its natural state."

Polly put her hands on the metal railing and stared out at the Mississippi River. "We believe it's a cascade failure, possibly due to a power fluctuation from the paranormal nuclear meltdown your father created."

Blah, blah, blah. Sere had no patience for technical babble. "Or maybe it's an evil genius in hell manipulating the dimension so he can help the doppelgängers escape and attack the living."

Polly turned toward Sere. "The professor isn't willing to entertain that option at the moment. He thinks he can take care of the problem from here."

"Meanwhile, I have to hunt down more of these manipulated demons and try to save the world from an all-out invasion."

Polly took Sere's hands. "I've known you most of your life. There are no hands I'd rather put the fate of the world in than yours. You've got your mission, and we have ours."

SERE WALKED AWAY from the shipping offices, seething, with the single piece of paper crumpled in her hand. *The professor is an arrogant prick. I fucking know my mission. And I don't need you acting like some corporate boss giving a pep talk to her assistant.*

Despite her frustration, Sere knew that Polly hadn't meant to be dismissive of her conviction that someone in hell was tweaking the program. Polly had simply been trying to protect the old scientist by backing his theories.

The day is going to come when Professor Yates can't maintain that equipment. What kind of hell will be turned loose then? Even if Polly can take over, someday that virtual projection is going to get out of hand, if it hasn't already.

Sere got back on her motorcycle and kicked the engine

over, hoping the physical act would shut off her insecurities. *Nothing I can do about hell's structure. Time to find out what happened to Fisher.* She consulted the page one last time before folding it up and slipping it under the cleavage of her bustier.

She kept her eyes peeled for the black Jeep Cherokee as she rode down the boisterous streets of the Bywater. *At least these people don't turn in early, but I'm going to have to keep a move on if I expect anyone to open their door to me after dinner.*

The shotgun double painted in bright shades of red and purple didn't look like the type of dwelling that would house someone in need of a CPA. It was more reminiscent of the kind of place where members of Kendell's old band—Polly Urethane and the Strippers—would have lived. Sere pounded on the door, not convinced that the loose wiring of the doorbell wouldn't spark a fire.

The trumpet softly playing a blues number Sere didn't recognize stopped, and the door opened. A black man in his early thirties stood in the doorway, still holding his instrument as if it were a part of his hand. "Can I help you?"

Sere had the same feeling of guilt she'd experienced on first meeting Fisher. *You've got a demon coming for you, and you don't even know it.* "I'm just following up on my boss's visit with you earlier today... Montgomery Fisher, CPA? He wanted to make sure you had this." She offered the man one of Fisher's cards.

The musician looked at it in confusion. "I'm sorry, I've never heard of this guy. No one's stopped by. I would have known as I've been practicing all day. Got a gig in an hour at the Blue Nile." He reached for the side table and handed her a card of his own.

Damn it. Why do you have to be so nice? Just once, I'd like to meet a fuck-face real so I don't have any feelings of obligation.

She pocketed the card. "Thanks. If I get through with my errands, I'll try to make it. And if my boss does stop by, would you let him know I was on the job?" She gave him the shared-suffering wink of service personnel.

He smiled and nodded. "You got it. Have a better evening." He had the trumpet back to his lips before the door had fully closed.

Strike one. Damn it, Fisher. Where the hell are you? Sidekicks aren't supposed to go on missions alone.

She got back on her bike for the ride to the Treme to confront the second name on her list, but before she could kick-start the engine, a vintage black VW bus blocked her exit. "Get in."

Damn it, Myles. "Can't," she said. "I've got something I need to do. I'll stop by for a visit sometime tomorrow." *Like I've got time for fake-family obligations.*

Kendell leaned over Myles from the passenger's seat. "We know you're searching for Montgomery Fisher, but you're not going to find him. He's been abducted."

You have to be kidding me. Sere started up the motorcycle. "I'll follow you."

Myles shook his head. "We need to talk before we get there. Your bike will be safe here."

How would you know? Sere squeezed her eyes shut in frustration. Once the pair got something in their heads, they'd never let it go no matter how many people they endangered.

"Fine." She shut off the motorcycle and wrapped her snakes around her neck before heading to the old bus. "How did you find me?"

Kendell reached behind her and opened the grindy sliding door. "Your spies are my spies, but that's not what's important right now—finding Mr. Fisher is. I've had someone keeping an eye on that kindly CPA since the day we found you and Bart saving him from his doppelgänger out in the swamp."

Sere climbed in and shut the door. "What did your homeless contingent tell you?"

"Like you, Mr. Fisher was heading out to talk to the four reals."

How did you figure out about the newly escaped demons? Oh, fuck it. You probably just talked to Professor Yates.

"How many did he meet?" Sere asked.

"Hard to say. The homeless aren't exactly mobile. One guy saw him leave his offices earlier than normal, and another found his Jeep in a dirt lot near the Industrial Canal. The hood was still warm and the doors unlocked, but nothing inside had been disturbed. My guy hung around in case Mr. Fisher had just stepped out to take a leak. Of course, that wasn't the case, but people on the street have a different reality from those who spend their lives in homes and offices. I often have to translate what the destitute see into what someone more economically stable would notice."

"And you came up with Fisher being abducted? Sounds like a stretch."

"Not when you consider that the warehouse Thomas took you to is only half a dozen blocks away from the dirt lot."

Shit. Sere leaned forward on the seat. "How fast can this jalopy go?"

"We're almost there," Myles said.

The couple had their skills when it came to the paranormal, but covert attack wasn't one of them. "Park next to the Jeep, away from the warehouse," Sere said. If Thomas was holding Fisher, she needed to get a look at what was going on between the two demon-possessed individuals before she would know for sure who to trust and who to watch out for.

EVEN FROM HALF A MILE AWAY, the abandoned warehouse gave Sere the creeps. Old homes ravaged by hurricanes lined the pothole-strewn street opposite to where they'd parked. Tractor-trailer rigs idled along the side of the road, waiting to take on their loads. *This is no place for Kendell and Myles*, she thought. *They're just going to get hurt out here.*

Kendell hunched down behind the black Jeep as if she thought Thomas had enhanced vision. "What do we do?"

The dirt lot appeared to be overflow parking for the still-functioning half dozen warehouses along the railroad tracks. "Thomas will be watching the front of the warehouse," Sere said. "He's not going to make the same mistake as before by leaving it unprotected. I'll need to approach from the back."

Myles held a pair of binoculars to his eyes. "Between the wire fences and security cameras, the warehouses aren't leaving a lot to chance. There's not much between the back of those buildings and the floodwall. I suppose we could work our way down along the batture. There is an opening in the wall for off-loading ships halfway down, but we'd still have to scale the wall first to get there."

The low rumble under Sere's feet made the VW's body panels rattle. "Train's coming. Stay low and keep up. We need to get across the tracks before the engineer sees us." Sere ran off toward the thick brush at the edge of the lot before either Myles or Kendell could respond. Nettles and creepers clawed at her arms and tore at her thin leggings, but she was through the thicket before the locomotive had reached the bend in the tracks. Without checking on Myles or Kendell, she scaled the twelve-foot wire fence and jumped down the other side.

"I can't make that," Kendell said.

No shit. "Did you bring any weapons?" Sere asked.

"No. During the one session we had with Joe, he made it clear we shouldn't carry anything that could be used against us."

Brilliant. No doubt, Joe was right, but how are these two supposed to defend themselves? "I assume you do have a cell phone. When I get clear, call Polly."

"Why do you want her?" Myles asked.

"I need someone with a field technology med kit— someone who's got the guts to use it." *And because I don't trust the professor,* she added to herself.

"Exactly what kind of trouble do you plan on getting yourself into?" Kendell asked.

I'll bet she's just dying to add "young lady" to that question.

"If I'm right, things are about to get ugly in there," Sere said. "With both men possessed by energy created in hell, we're going to need more than bandages once this is over." She didn't need to waste any more time discussing possibilities. "Give me fifteen minutes, then run the half mile to the warehouse. I'll try to distract Thomas so you can make your approach. Just don't enter the building until I give you the signal."

The train's three headlights lit the far side of the tracks, but the curve's embankment left enough of a shadow to easily hide a person. Sere sprinted over the tracks and lay flat on the coarse gravel. As the lights swung toward the warehouses, indicating that the train was rounding the corner, Kendell's worried face came into view just before Myles pulled her back into the bushes.

The smell of burnt diesel, the loud squeal of metal wheels against metal rail, and the sight of the towering locomotive made Sere lie even flatter on the ground. Hopefully, the people in the cab were more focused on bringing this monster alongside the correct warehouse than looking out for a stowaway. She waited until three of the tanker cars had passed before making her move. Once the front-wheel truck of the fourth car cleared her head, she scampered over the first rail and lay flat on the cement sleepers that supported the tracks. She reached up and latched onto the metal bars that ran the length of the tanker.

With one quick flexing of her arms, she was off the ground and against the bottom of the railcar.

She counted off the warehouses as the train passed the solid concrete loading bays. When it reached the abandoned warehouse, she let go of the metal support, dropped to the tracks, and rolled out from under the train. There was barely enough room between the guillotine of metal wheels on rails and cold, hard concrete wall. A loud screeching of brakes came from the locomotive. *Stage one complete.*

WITH THE MAIN loading bay door closed and chained shut, Sere checked each window along the back of the warehouse for a way into the building. *Somewhere there has to be a bathroom or back office in this damn structure.* Unfortunately, when Thomas had held her captive, she hadn't spent much time on the building's floor plan.

She ducked below a frosted-glass window and played her knife along the edge to find the latch. The window popped open. Instead of trying to squeeze through the tight opening, she fed the heads of the two snakes under the window.

"See anyone?" she hissed.

The snakes wriggled side to side before slithering over the frame and into the room. *No yelling. That's a good thing.* She hoisted herself up to the window and followed her companions over the edge.

The bathroom smelled as if it hadn't been cleaned in a decade. *Doesn't matter. I'm not staying here long.* She looked around the floor and fixtures, but her snakes had magically disappeared. *Now, where did you go?*

A hissing from above directed her attention to the acoustic-tiled ceiling. Poking out next to the tile-sized ventilation duct was one of the snakes. He wiggled his diamond-shaped head.

"Good thinking." She hopped up, grabbed the metal track that separated the crumbling pressed-board tiles, and followed her snake onto the warehouse's rafters. Old tarps, lighting fixtures from another era, and an array of garbage filled the storage space above the handful of shipping offices —all of it covered by a layer of dust so thick she feared she would sneeze if she moved too fast.

She crept along the structural metal grid that covered most of the warehouse floor space. Following the path her two snakes had marked out in the dust without being noticed by the men below required most of her attention. The sound of Fisher's voice made her go as still as a black panther stalking her prey. During a covert operation, surprise was a constant threat. She peeked over the edge. Instead of Thomas looming over Fisher as she'd expected, the tables were turned, and Thomas was the one strapped to the chair.

Fisher turned the red shotgun cartridge between his fingers in front of Thomas's face. "I want to talk to your demon."

"Why?" Thomas asked. The perpetually arrogant prick didn't appear to find the kindly CPA all that intimidating.

The professional businessman squeezed out a couple of paranormal pellets onto the metal desk in the otherwise empty warehouse. "Because you and I have something in common. Before I can determine if that's for our mutual good or destruction, however, I need a little more information." He took one of the stones between his fingers and pinched so hard that his face tensed from the pain. Even from twenty feet away, Sere could see the red overtake the whites of his eyes.

Fisher is fucking drawing forth his demon.

Thomas's eyes grew wide and red. He didn't need the stimulation for his own demon to rise to the surface. "What do you have in mind?" he growled in a voice more animal than human.

"Tell me what you know about the four demons headed this way. What is their mission?"

Thomas's smile reminded Sere of the doppelgänger she'd known as a little girl in hell. "What makes you think I know anything that you don't?"

Sere gripped the metal beam in frustration. *I'd chop his head off all over again if I had the chance.* Everything she saw took on the familiar red glow. *I have a soul. I don't have to give in to my temptations. But then, those two aren't empty shells either. We're not as different as I had imagined.*

Fisher eased up on the pressure of his fingers. Before Sere knew what was happening, he kicked the chair over, pinched Thomas's nose, and forced the paranormal pebble down his throat. "Swallow it," he grunted between clenched teeth.

Sere eased her grip on the rafter, curious about what was about to happen to the demon-possessed young man.

Thomas thrashed against his bonds like a man being drowned. "Turn me loose," he grunted.

With one hand still at Thomas's throat, Fisher reached up to the desk for a second pellet. "Tell me about the four demons."

"I don't know anything, you fuckface. Why would I?" Thomas, now the defiant demon-prick, wasn't all that different from the human version of himself.

"Because I know you're having dreams, just like I am."

Fuck. Why can't I ever learn to trust the right people? Fisher should have told me before going off half-cocked like this. She pulled the shotgun from her thigh holster and laid it on the rafter. If one little pellet could fully draw forth the demon in Thomas, a hole blasted through his chest with the little buggers just might end her problem with him.

The snake slithered over the stock of her gun and stared at her through the sights.

"Fine," she whispered. She took her finger off the trigger but left the gun lying on the beam. Not killing a human being still counted for something in what was left of her personal code. "But if he goes translucent, I'm shooting."

If fear was part of Thomas's makeup, he did a masterful job of covering it up with anger. "If you're having the same dreams, why pester me for answers?"

"The demon in me isn't as fully in command as in you. I'm betting that makes you even more susceptible to hell's edicts. At least tell me whose voice I'm hearing in my sleep."

"Maybe you should meet him yourself." Thomas lunged up from his chair—his zip-tie bonds cut with his switchblade. The quick action knocked Fisher on his back. His head bounced off the concrete floor.

Damn it! Sere's vision went demonic red as she swung down from the rafter with her bootheels aimed straight at Thomas's head. The memory of how Joe had escaped her direct attack made her add a body twist just as she let go of the beam. Like a human-sized rifle bullet, she corkscrewed her feet into Thomas's forehead, knocking him over the chair. Once clear of her adversary, she did a gymnastic handspring off the floor, stuck the landing, and stood with bent knees and knife in hand facing him.

Thomas came up bleeding but still holding his blade. "I should have known you'd be lurking around in the shadows. So you've resorted to sending your CPA to clean up your mess?"

"Doesn't everyone?" she asked.

He came at her with all the demonic fury she had experienced while fighting Joe in the swamp. He was full of unfocused rage, but he was still human.

Don't make the mistake of thinking he suffers from your doppelgänger shortcomings. She focused on her heartbeat to conserve her blood's oxygen. When he made his thrust at her abdomen, she sprang clear of his lunge and, halfway through a backflip, clocked him in the chin with the toe of her boot.

The instinct to kill, combined with her training, was a powerful intoxicant. He sliced at her in a street-fighting style more conducive to multiple attackers than one-on-one encounters. *Is this you, or is my true adversary trying out some multiplayer tactics before the big event?* She parried an especially determined move with a leg sweep, but Thomas's wild gesticulations made it hard for her to anticipate how and where he would land. As he fell, his blade slashed deep into her arm. He rolled clear of her counterattack before getting back to his feet.

The pain only increased her vision's red hues. Instead of waiting for him to formulate his next attack, she took a gymnastic tumbling run at him, each handspring and cartwheel designed to increase her momentum while keeping all options open regarding her ultimate strike. At a distance of six feet, she directed her force down into her knees then exploded up with fists together, aimed at his ugly demonic face. The hit was like a bowling ball crushing a lone remaining pin. Thomas flew backward and ricocheted off the office wall.

She should have felt victorious, but his position of vulnerability only fed her aggression. "I'm going to kill you." Her words were so filled with animal instinct that she wasn't sure they'd come from her or from some creature lurking within.

The sounds of her snakes slithering above attracted her attention just as her shotgun fell into her hands from the rafter. She cocked all four hammers and aimed the barrels at Thomas's chest.

"Is this your answer for curing me of my demon?" Bloody and dazed, he struggled to his feet.

Both snakes uncurled from above and landed on her shoulders. Her hands flexed on the shotgun as if unwilling to accept the humanity that struggled to overcome her demonic desire. The red hues softened to yellows and oranges. "Go now." She couldn't trust herself to move, for fear the muscle memory of battle might return.

He bolted for the door, knocking Kendell and Myles on their asses as they busted in. *I hope that wasn't their idea of a stealthy entrance.* The pair didn't even try to stop Thomas but instead raced for the man laid out unconscious on the floor.

"What took you so long?" Sere asked.

Kendell crouched next to Fisher. "You told us to wait fifteen minutes then watch for your signal. When we heard the commotion, we gave up sitting on the sidelines." She pressed her fingers to his wrist. "He's still got a pulse, but there's blood under his head. We need to call 9-1-1."

"Where's Polly?" In her post-demonic state, Sere found it hard to form more than simple questions.

Myles stood over Kendell as if there was still some danger that demanded his protection. "We called her as soon as you rolled under the train. She should be here shortly."

Damn that time thing again. I'll bet the whole fight didn't last five minutes. "We need to wait until she gets here."

Kendell looked up in alarm. "Why? Are you hurt too?"

Sere's ability to speak slowly overcame her animal instincts. She turned her arm to inspect Thomas's single victory. "It's just a scratch. I'm fine, but Fisher called forth his demon before dealing with Thomas. If he goes straight to the hospital, I'm not sure who will come out of the coma."

"Fuck it all to hell."

Sere had never heard Kendell swear before.

"I'M HERE," Polly yelled from the warehouse entrance. She lugged the oversized backpack on her shoulder over to Fisher and dropped it next to Kendell.

"You have to hook him up to the projection." Sere's pulse was increasing. *What the hell? The battle is over. Why am I getting amped up now?*

Polly shook her head. "Unlike you, he's human, not doppelgänger. Nothing would happen. The bandage reinforces the connection to the real. Since this *is* Mr. Fisher, it wouldn't do any good."

That's where you're wrong. Fisher is in a lot more danger than you know, she thought. But anything she told Polly would inevitably get back to the professor, and Sere wasn't ready to trust the old man with information that sensitive. "Just trust me and do it."

Polly picked up one of the pellets from the desk. "Tell me you didn't try something stupid. If he has one of these things inside him, the bandage could pull it through his body, creating all sorts of damage."

Thanks for the vote of confidence. I'm not that stupid. But arguing with Polly wasn't going to help the CPA at their feet, so Sere got right to the point. "It wasn't me. Fisher forced one of those little pebbles down Thomas's throat. That's how he went all demonic."

Polly turned the small pellet between her fingers. "Interesting."

"Look, I'll tell you all the fun little tricks I've learned to do with these shiny rocks another time. We don't have time for curiosity right now."

Polly was still staring at the shotgun pellet while Sere started ransacking the medical bag.

"The technological bandage will work. I'm well acquainted with the spiritual mechanics. Lord knows, I've gotten into Jennifer's mind often enough. The professor said that even if she died, he had enough information on her in his memory banks to resurrect me no matter what mischief I got into." She pulled out what seemed like a mile of cloth bandage. "If he's got any information at all on Montgomery Fisher, the connection should work to remind this sweet man of who he is. I don't need to repair his body. I need to fix his soul. Once we're sure he is still the kindly CPA, we can call in the paramedics."

Polly finally got her ass in gear and started wrapping the cloth around Fisher's head. "If he's unconscious, how do you expect to know who's in charge?"

"Because you're going to hardwire him to me."

"What?" all three yelled at once.

Sere uncoiled the connecting cable. "The professor's equipment is geared toward me, and I am a doppelgänger living in reality. Think of me as a power converter."

Polly handed Sere a role of bandage. "This is wildly dangerous. I'm only agreeing to it because I don't see another option."

"I can see about a dozen options," Kendell said. "Like take him to the hospital first and deal with what comes out of him later. Hooking you up to a person just seems like a disaster waiting to happen."

Like it hasn't already happened? Sere ripped at the end of the second bandage to expose the wires, resisting the urge to waste more time arguing with Kendell. She held the bare ends in one hand and the computer cord in the other. *Now what?*

"Give it to me." Polly fished around in her backpack and came up with a handful of connections that looked like computer intestines.

"Is no one listening to me?" Kendell asked. "This is a bad idea. I'm calling the paramedics."

Good luck. Sere stared at her, waiting to witness the loss-of-signal irritation that anyone who tried to use a wireless device around Sere suffered. "This isn't a democracy. When it comes to the mechanics of hell or dealings with the devil, you're the expert. But we're talking about battles of the soul now, and that's not something you understand." She didn't mean to be harsh, but wasting time was one of Kendell's weaknesses, whether she knew it or not, and this simply wasn't the moment for it.

Myles put his hand on Kendell's back. "I'm sorry, my love, but Sere is right."

Kendell seemed about to argue her case until she looked into his eyes. "I sometimes forget you've been there too. Baron Malveaux's possession of your body seems like a lifetime ago."

Sere wrapped the jerry-rigged bandage around her head like a bandana. "What is with you people and reliving history?"

Polly finished preparing Fisher, connected the two bandages with the spaghetti-noodle computer intestines, and plugged Sere's bandage into the phone cord. Then she looked over at Kendell and Myles. "There should be just enough line to run this out the front door. From there, one of you should be able to call into the professor's equipment." She held up the med kit's phone. "There's only one application. All you need to do is tap the icon. I need to stay here and keep an eye on our patients."

Kendell got up from Fisher's side. "Since my ideas are apparently not of any use, I might as well do something productive."

Myles went with her like an attentive bodyguard.

"You might want to lie down," Polly said. "This has never been done before, and I don't have a way of keeping tabs on what's going to happen. As this is your idea, have you got any suggestions?"

Wow, we really must be in uncharted territory for you to ask me for advice. Sere took off her analog military wristwatch and set it on the concrete floor next to her ear. "I suck at time, but I should be able to hear the ticking even if I'm inside Fisher's head." She thought back to her connections with Jennifer. "Give me five minutes."

Polly sat close enough to see the watch. "I'll give you three, then I'm pulling the plug."

THE WORST PART about being in someone else's head was identifying which were her own thoughts, which theirs, and which were the oddly new collaborative ideas. Usually, she could rely on her level of cursing as a good measure of who was doing the thinking. If "fuck" wasn't used in every other sentence, she could be reasonably sure it was the host brain doing the processing. Jennifer, after all, was a mom trying to set a good example in thoughts as well as deeds for her young son. When dealing with a partially demon-possessed consciousness, however, all bets were off.

"I'm going to take over and fucking burn this godforsaken reality to the ground. Hell keeps sending minions like damned moths to the flame. How shitty does a leader have to be to keep sacrificing his warriors in pursuit of a lone little girl? I'll stand at the gate to hell and welcome my brothers and sisters to their rightful place. Fucking see if I don't."

Okay, not me. I'd never refer to myself like that. "Badass demon killer" maybe, but never "little girl."

"You are truly a fool. Even at my most negative and desperate, I never considered destroying the world. Emotional pain is the result of separation from people, and furthering that divide only makes things worse. You'd turn that suffering into a permanent condition."

The argument between the two masculine spirits that were nearly identical in energy signature made Sere dizzy. Images began fluttering around her awareness like flowers falling off a magnolia tree. *Pretty*, she thought. She focused on the closest one, which expanded into a memory.

Annabelle Campbell's perfectly piercing green eyes cut through the smoky nightclub on Bourbon Street like a high-intensity strobe light. But instead of lighting up the customers crammed onto the noisy dance floor, they penetrated straight into Montgomery Fisher's heart. He was certain all the men in the club instantly fell for her the moment the singer's eyes passed over their faces. Her gaze finally settled on him, and she smiled. At that very moment, he knew he would marry her. He'd have asked her then and there—in front of all the dancing, sweating, drunk partiers —if he hadn't feared scaring her off.

At thirty-one, he was just leaving the painfully shy stage of his life. His parents attributed his lack of a wife to his being a late bloomer. The seersucker suit and purple bow tie had been his attempt at crafting a cover identity to hide his insecurities. The image meshed well with his pursuit of an advanced degree in mathematics, though the combination had resulted in even his closest friends labeling him a nerd. With nothing to lose, he chose to embrace the title and hoped he would one day find a mousy little undergrad willing to be swept away by his intelligence and genteel nature.

Never in all his years had he expected to attract a woman with a beauty approaching that of Annabelle. Twenty years, ten months, and fourteen days later, he still couldn't believe that first premonition had come to pass.

Sere let the flower-petal memory drift back on the wind of consciousness. "Gummy, I think my water just broke." The next fragrant petal that covered Sere's awareness was so powerful she felt her heart rush as she ran into the downstairs bedroom. Sweet, lovely, radiant Ann—she'd insisted on the shortened name when she'd accepted Fisher as her last name—lay sweating and panting on the guest bed.

"What do I do?" Being cool in a crisis was one thing, but

seeing his wife in distress blew away any male reserve Montgomery could muster. Her anguish was his kryptonite.

And her smile was his salvation. "Come here and help me up. Thank goodness you had the foresight to move me to the guest bedroom. Can you imagine trying to get me down those stairs with this humongous belly?" She was trying to calm him, and he knew it. It worked.

"I've got you."

The bright-red flower was sucked away from Sere as if by a hurricane. In its place, a young girl in petticoats ran through a field of wildflowers. *Wait. That's me.*

Sere felt as if her eyes were being ripped out of her face. "Fucking ouch!"

"That's three minutes," Polly said. Her voice was like fingernails on a chalkboard.

Sere rubbed her temples, fearful of pressing any closer to her eyes. "You simply have to modify that app so I don't feel like my insides are being torn apart each time you turn off the connection."

"Weren't you listening to the watch?"

"I forgot." *More like I was distracted by being in someone else's memories.* Now that she was back in her own doppelgänger body, she knew that the final memory she'd witnessed wasn't from Montgomery Fisher. It wasn't from Jennifer Cranston either. The memory belonged to Serephine Malveaux, and there was no way the professor could have had that version of her on file. Someone—either an entity from hell or the loas of the dead—was too close. *Please let it be an entity from hell.*

Kendell came back into the warehouse while Myles

stood outside the door, cell phone in hand. "*Now* can we call the paramedics?"

"Gummy—I mean Montgomery—is spiritually fine. He's got a lot more of an emotional foundation than I'd suspected." She looked down at the unresponsive CPA. "Time to get him fixed up so he can get back to those who love him."

SERE HUDDLED next to Kendell in the early-morning light as the ambulance pulled out of the crumbling parking lot. "Take me back to my motorcycle. I need to get to the hospital."

"We'll go with you," Kendell said. "You can use the van to stash your shotgun and snakes." She looked Sere over like a mother analyzing her child's back-to-school wardrobe. "A change of clothing wouldn't be the worst idea either. I only wore that steampunk getup during Halloween gigs. You do realize it's supposed to have a dress with it? Only Polly wore costumes that revealing. We could swing by the condo on the way."

Not happening. One time wearing a sundress was enough. "Just trying to fit in." Sere didn't want to cap off a night of fighting with an argument about her attire.

Polly threw the paranormal med kit into the back of the VW bus. "A lead singer needs to stand out. Besides, we were making a statement about taking back our sexual identities. Don't get all conservative on me now, *Olympia Stain*. Sere looks fine. We need to get to the hospital right now, no detours. I don't trust that the medical professionals won't mess up our emergency soul treatment. Between the anesthesia, antibiotics, and lord knows what else, Fisher might end up weak enough that his evil twin reasserts himself."

Though the prospect of having everyone sitting around the waiting room in case a demon started tearing through the hospital wasn't ideal, Sere knew she was outnumbered. "Fine. I just want to get there before his family does. They shouldn't have to sit around wondering what happened to him. Since he didn't come home last night, they're probably already in a state of panic." The pang in her heart—left over from her psychic bond with Gummy—made her accept leaving her motorcycle behind.

Myles cranked the grumpy VW engine to life. "I'll run you all to the hospital first. As soon as we find out Fisher's condition, Kendell and I will start to work on damage control. We're going to need Joe to intercept any police report that might have gotten filed regarding last night's activities, and we can retrieve your motorcycle."

Kendell's tensed muscles and increased breathing betrayed her excitement. "You don't mind me driving it again, do you?"

Do you have any idea how much you sound like a teenager bouncing for joy at getting the keys to the family car? Sere pulled the key with attached alligator-tooth fob out of her leather bustier. "Just don't go hot-rodding around town."

The old bus never was particularly fast, but hearing the poor little engine strain to push the big metal box up onto the freeway made Sere wonder if she wouldn't have been better off walking. *Why aren't we there yet?*

For distraction, she turned to Polly, who was sitting next to her. "Why were you so interested in the shotgun pellet?"

The woman had a similar lost-in-thought expression to the professor's when something was vexing her. "The only thing that material is supposed to do is cut a doppelgänger off from its real's projection. Since Thomas no longer has a double—in hell or otherwise—the pebble shouldn't have had any effect, but even Fisher must have known something would happen, or he wouldn't have made Thomas swallow it."

She decided to share what she knew about the pellets, even if Polly did end up telling Sere's secrets to the professor. Some problems needed smarter brains to solve. "The swamp creatures come running when I toss a paranormal shell in the water. And though a boat isn't animal in nature, I was able to coax an unresponsive motor back to life by dropping pellets in the gas tank."

Polly nodded as if an idea was forming and she was attempting to tap it into place. "They must be working as some kind of feedback loop. Whatever is currently being picked up by the professor's equipment—instead of being sent into hell—is being projected back into the original model."

Sere never could follow Polly when she started talking science. "Stop being my teacher, and tell me what's going on."

"Sorry, I'm just talking the idea out, not lecturing. If animals, human or otherwise, had their own energy fed back to them, it would make them more present in the moment. Like, seeing what's happening not just with their eyes but with their spirits as well."

Sere struggled to keep up. "You mean like déjà vu?"

"Not quite. They wouldn't experience a time change in what they saw. More like omnipresence."

Myles turned his head sideways to butt into the conversation from the driver's seat. "Sounds like dipping a toe in the *deep waters.*"

"That wouldn't explain Thomas's reaction, though," Polly yelled over the engine noise. "If he is possessed by the spirit of his doppelgänger, those evil intentions might be what was being manifested."

Sere settled back on the seat, wondering what would have happened to Fisher if he'd taken one of the pellets. *Would the physical damage become worse? Could he have focused on his family and pulled himself out of his connection to his demon?* Once again, it appeared that the professor had made something he had no control over.

THE NURSE CAME out of the emergency room and told the group that it would be a while before they knew anything.

"That's my cue to leave," Kendell said before heading back out to join Myles in the bus.

Just as well, Sere thought. *The last thing I need is a mother figure thinking I need emotional support.* The waiting room made no sense at all to her. "Why won't they let us in?" she asked Polly.

"Doesn't work that way. Doctors like to work in private. Someone will come out when they know something."

Convenient. If something goes wrong, there's no one to see. "But why is it taking so long? Can't they just hook up a monitor and figure out what's wrong with him?"

Polly had the irritating smile of a mother who simultaneously wanted to tell her child to shut up and sympathized with her impatience. "It's the way things work."

That's a bullshit answer if there ever was one. Sere stopped pacing in front of the painting of a forest in fall and sat on the orange fabric bench. Her heart caught in her throat when she saw the three women push their way through the wood-paneled swinging doors.

"Sit here, you two. I'll go find out what's happening."

Sere's legs were wobbly as she stood. "Annabelle?" *Fuck, she goes by Ann now!*

"I'm Ann Fisher."

Fisher was wrong about one thing: it isn't just men who fall for her eyes when she locks her gaze on them. "I'm Sere Mal-Laurette. I work with your husband."

The strained lines around the woman's eyes and mouth quivered as if she were about to break down. "Can you tell me what happened?"

Sere wondered how much Ann Fisher could handle. "It's a long story, but it ends with me being too slow to stop the asshole from pushing Mr. Fisher backward onto the concrete floor." Sere caught the look of the two late-teenage girls behind their mother. "Sorry about my language."

HELL BENT FOR DEMONS

"It's okay," Ann said. "I'd have used a lot worse. What was he doing in an abandoned warehouse?"

So she knew about the warehouse already. *The paramedics must have called in a report. Damn people and their rapid communications.*

"That's the long part of the story. Your husband is very brave but a little overly chivalrous." Sere hoped she had read Fisher's insight correctly. Part of what had swept Ann into Montgomery's arms was his old-fashioned ideas about looking after the woman he loved.

Ann's eyes closed only partially as they swept Sere from head to toe. "What is your relationship to Montgomery?"

I saved his life but am responsible for him being possessed by a demon. Yeah, that should go over well. "He helped me with a particularly vexing life-or-death problem," Sere said.

Ann shook her head. "Everyone says that. He's an accountant, for pity's sake. From the way his clients go on about how relieved they are for his help, you'd think he was some kind of superhero."

If you only knew. "I'm still not sure why he agreed to let me work with him."

By raising two daughters, Ann Fisher had further developed her penetrating stare. What had begun as the strobe-light attraction Montgomery first noticed had been refined into a laser able to cut away falsehood. *Damn. I'll bet those girls never pull anything over on her.*

"That still doesn't explain what you two were doing in a dirty warehouse in the middle of the night, fighting off some hoodlum."

"Not all of my clients are good, upstanding citizens."

Now, there's an understatement. "Mr. Fisher wasn't willing to let me face this one alone. Unfortunately, he got to the meeting before I did." *Might have helped if he'd clued me in to what he was up to.*

"Sounds like my husband." Ann finally took a seat. "I assume no one's come out yet?"

Sere gratefully sat next to the woman. "Not yet. The paramedics just brought him in a little while ago. He was semiconscious before they got to us." She hoped a change of topic would take some of the edge off. "Please tell me to bug off if my question is too personal"—Sere caught herself at the last minute from using her usual expletive—"but why *Gummy?*"

Ann's softly feminine laugh was nearly as captivating as her eyes. "When we first started dating, he was so sweet it was nearly sickening, so I started calling him my gummy bear. He hated it. Later in our relationship, there was a period when I wasn't the most faithful. I didn't cheat on him, but being a singer in nightclubs, I let my flirting get the better of me. He clung to me like a gummy bear stuck in my teeth. He simply wouldn't let go. I realized at that point how good he truly was. He'd never leave me."

The younger of the two daughters leaned over her mother. "Only Mom gets to call him that, but we each buy him a bag of gummy bears for his birthday. It's our family's little inside joke." The daughter didn't have her mother's sophisticated stare, but with her direct eye contact, soft voice, and attentive listening style, she had a similarly captivating demeanor.

Sere turned back to Ann. "He's madly in love with you and always has been."

The woman's eyes glistened. "I know. He's one of the good ones, and there aren't many of his kind left."

A man in scrubs came down the hall to the nearly deserted waiting room. "Mrs. Fisher?"

"I'm Ann." She stood up and tensed her body as if bracing for a storm surge.

"Your husband is going to be just fine. He has a concussion, but by all indications, he won't suffer any long-term damage. I'd like to keep him here for twenty-four hours, though, just to keep an eye on him."

Sere wanted to talk with Fisher. She needed to find out how he'd located Thomas, what he'd discovered about the four doppelgängers headed her way, and what the hell he was thinking going out on his own. The tears the three Fisher women were no longer able to control, however, convinced Sere that now wasn't the time.

She put her hand on Ann's shoulder. "He should have his family with him. I'll head to the office and let Linda know he won't be in today. Tell him not to worry about anything." *Thomas and the other four fuckers are mine.*

As Ann and her daughters headed down the hall to see Fisher, Sere turned to Polly. "I've got things I need to do."

Polly smiled and nodded. "Yes, you do. Kendell texted that she dropped off your motorcycle, but they couldn't wait around. I'll stay here in case there's an update on Fisher's condition."

And to be sure he doesn't go all demony. Of the available

support group, Polly would be the best able to handle any possibility.

Sere pulled out one of the CPA's business cards from her bustier. "Call the office if there's any news, but if it's bad, don't tell Linda, the receptionist."

"Got it." Polly pocketed the card.

Outside the hospital, Sere took a deep breath of the fresh, humid, unfiltered air. At first, she was relieved to see her motorcycle parked in front with her saddlebags draped over the back. *But where are my fucking knife and gun?* She hopped on and kicked the engine over. *Probably Kendell's way of getting me to stop by for a chat. I guess now's as good a time as any.* She checked her watch. *8:23 a.m. I'll swing by the office to let Linda know Fisher won't be in then head over to Kendell and Myles's condo.*

KENDELL WOULD HAVE A ZILLION QUESTIONS—SHE always did—and answering them to the woman's satisfaction usually took way more time than Sere could afford. *Maybe if I start asking questions, we can wrap this up quickly.*

"What's the damage-control update?"

Kendell sat on the couch with her ancient dog on her lap. "Joe is in contact with the police down here. He thinks he can squash any report that might spring up. A person being knocked unconscious during a fight in New Orleans isn't exactly big news."

"Did he have anything to say about the demons up

north?" *Those bastards must be getting a little soggy out in the swamp for so long.*

"Nothing yet. It's only been two days since you were up there."

Fuck. Is that all? Time flies when you're hunting demons. Seeing those green flashes seems like a lifetime ago.

"He did ask if we'd talked about your theory of one dead to one demon," Kendell added.

"It's not really a theory—more of an observation. Monty killed seven people before I was able to catch him. Then seven doppelgängers escaped hell. Joe taught me to be suspicious of coincidences."

"And rightly so." Kendell's eyes glazed over the way Polly's did when she was considering some bit of evidence she'd just as soon ignore. "If a demon from our hell dimension left that reality and killed someone here, I wonder what would happen to the real person's soul. You haven't had any whiff of the loas of the dead, have you?"

"Thankfully, no." *Shit. You're wondering if they even know about the deaths.* "Please tell me you don't suspect those souls are ending up in hell."

Kendell smiled as if she were trying to calm a frightened child. "I'm sure it's nothing to worry about. Capturing your father was no easy feat. Souls don't just fall into the hellmouth on their own."

Sere was completely sure that it was something to worry about, but the last thing she wanted to do was attract the attention of the loas of the dead. "Even if there is a correlation, if I can stop the remaining four doppelgängers before they start killing, I might be able to stem the tide."

"While you're doing that, I'll check with my sources on the situation of these misplaced souls." Kendell bit her lip and hesitated then asked, "Any word from Sanguine?"

Sanguine was probably the only one who would know for sure if Larry, Kelly, and the rest were among the damned. If so, Sere hoped she was looking out for them. But relying on the guardian angel who'd raised her yet somehow failed to prevent the demons escaping hell seemed like a pipe dream.

"I tried sending a message, but we don't exactly have an interdimensional communication network."

Kendell petted her old dog and nodded. "Reopening the gates we created could alert the loas. Sanguine never was one for accepting a call unless it suited her needs, anyway."

For a change, Sere found herself in the position of comfort giver. "I trust Sanguine completely. If she were in trouble, she'd get word to me."

Kendell smiled but refrained from responding.

No more questions? Fuck yeah! Sere got up and grabbed her knife and shotgun off the coffee table. "I'll be hanging close to Fisher's offices until he gets back on his feet. Linda's sweet but not very good when it comes to making up excuses."

10

"Miss Sere, your four o'clock appointment is here." The voice from the intercom made Sere drop the shotgun shell she was loading, spilling the small metal pellets all over the desk.

That woman can't possibly be this senile. She squeezed her eyes shut in an attempt at tapping down her irritation and pressed the brittle plastic bar. "I don't have a four o'clock appointment, Linda. I'm not a real CPA."

She knew she should cut the receptionist a break. After all, her boss was laid up in the hospital. Since Sere had only worked there for less than two days, it was understandable that the woman would assume she was just another temp.

"I know that, dear. He says you were recommended to him."

Sere swept the metal pellets into the top drawer of her desk. *I suppose I don't need a normal shotgun shell just yet. It's not like Thomas is going to show his ugly face so soon after his last whooping. I could use the distraction.*

"Fine. Send him in." Sere checked the handle of the knife in her boot to be sure it was conveniently within reach.

She got up as a man roughly her age—at least the age she projected—entered her office, looking as uncomfortable as a schoolboy called to the principal's office. She was reminded of Fisher's description of meeting a new client. Many had a look of floundering desperation combined with a longing for someone to understand their plight.

"Evert Thibodaux," he said, reaching out his hand.

She gave him the firm single-pump handshake of a professional businessperson. "I'm not sure what I can do for you, but let's start with the basics. How did you hear about me and the firm?"

He took the brown vinyl-cushioned metal chair opposite her without it being offered. *You're used to being the one in charge, aren't you?* She engaged her combat training. Something about the guy didn't fit the frightened-customer persona he'd used to get past the receptionist and gain access to her office.

"Rampart said I should look for the CPA's office when I got down here."

Sere hadn't met so many people in life that she would forget a name like that. "I don't know anyone by that name."

"Sorry. He said you'd know him as Bart."

That's his fucking name? It fits. Stalwart bulkhead or macho prick? Rambart, more like it. Ramming his Bart into every woman he meets.

She tried to pull it together and keep her tone light. "If Bart sent you, I'm guessing this isn't in regard to your taxes."

"It's not," the man said, not cracking a smile. "I'm Ram's cousin. He might have mentioned me."

Shit—the cop. "Do you mind if I continue to call him Bart?"

"You can call him Asshole for all I care. We may be kin, but every time I see him, bad things seem to follow."

Sere didn't see any point in delaying the obvious. "Is this about Larry and Kelly's murders?"

"Not directly, but if you return to Opelousas Parish, I'm sure the sheriff would like to have a chat. Sheriff Newton doesn't know I'm here."

Sere fingered the butt of her knife. "Then why *are* you here?"

"Desperation. After you left our parish, a dozen hunters ventured into the deep swamp, and only three returned. We're conducting a search, of course, but that's mostly a formality to pacify the lost men's families."

Who took them—Lefty and his alligators or the demons I haven't found yet?

"What makes you think I'd know anything about the goings-on of a bunch of gator hunters?" she asked.

"I'm just following up on Ram's recommendation. He said you were raised by a swamp witch and knew the area better than anyone else. Do you have any idea why the hunters would risk losing their licenses by venturing so far from their established grounds in the middle of the night?"

Sere hoped her shrug of disinterest was convincing.

"There have always been tales of monster-sized gators lurking where the hunters can't reach them."

"This doesn't seem like greed. Nearly all of the hunters tag out every season. Though there is a pride aspect in bringing home the biggest catch, they've never so wantonly risked their necks when easier prey is within their grasp."

If those assholes had run across the four missing demons, at least the dumb fucks were providing enough entertainment to distract hell's army from heading into town. *But damn*, she thought, *that's a lot of new openings for future doppelgängers.*

"You said the official answer is they got lost," she said. "Sounds plausible to me."

He pulled three police files from his briefcase and tossed them onto her desk. "According to the three survivors, the other nine men are dead."

Shit. She nodded at the files. "I'm sure whoever took their statements was either a friend or relative. So tell me what I *won't* find in those pages."

"Ram said you were a smart cookie. I interviewed the men myself, and I've known each of them since high school —not that they attended. All three were in varying states of shock. That's pretty unusual for men who spend their lives out on the water. I've seen a guy get his hand bitten off and still land the gator like nothing happened. Their initial explanation of a band of alligators working in unison against the hunters wasn't that strange. There always seems to be some monster who's lived so long that he gets good at avoiding being caught. Expanding that legend to make it about a group of gators who can coordinate their efforts wouldn't take much imagination. The animal's thirty-foot leader, however, crosses from swamp lore to tall tale."

More like long tail. Sere did her best to suppress her giggle, but from the deputy's grimace, she could tell she hadn't been completely successful.

"I'm guessing you're familiar with the next part of my story," he continued. "The hunters talked of a short, squirrelly, redheaded swamp witch who commanded the thirty-foot gator like a pet puppy. Between their story and some rumors of bar brawls, I'm beginning to wonder if I should have shown up to this meeting with my gun and a search warrant."

Sere took her hand off her knife and settled back into her chair. The fact that Deputy Thibodaux had shown up unarmed indicated that he was open to having a cooperative relationship, despite all of his misgivings about her. "There's no need for that. I did confront the hunters and warn them against going too deep into the swamp." Sere was never any good at lying, so she simply left out the part about her riding on Lefty's back.

"Ram said I could trust you, so I'm not going to go into interrogation mode, but you have to see how my boss is eventually going to come looking for you. Most of what the three men had to say about you was conveniently left out of the official reports, but keeping your story quiet wasn't easy. The files on your desk are my original unedited notes."

Bart must have pulled some strings awfully hard to keep her out of the spotlight. *Fuck. Now I owe that Ramp bastard.*

"So far," she said, "the hunters' stories sound like they

could be discounted to dehydration and too long of a day in the swamp."

"Maybe so, but I'm also still looking for answers regarding these two individuals who passed through town a couple of months ago." He pulled out two folded police sketches from his pocket and spread them out on her desk.

She immediately recognized the drawings and inwardly cursed.

He held up the one resembling her. "I'm no expert, but this looks a hell of a lot like you. And this other one resembles the picture of this establishment's head CPA that's hanging in the lobby. Mind explaining the resemblances?"

"I thought they solved the Swamp Strangler case." By intercepting communications between the parish sheriff's office and the New Orleans police department, Joe had been able to convince each that the other had solved the case. The flimsy resolution only held up so long as no one from one force checked in with someone from the other.

The deputy looked at the drawings as if he expected to find something new. "Supposedly, some body parts were found in the Lafitte preserve down here that matched DNA found at Kelly's Diner."

"You still have your doubts?" Sere silently willed the man to be as simpleminded as his Northshore brethren.

"I worked that crime scene. It was messy. The serial killer made a hack job of it, so finding his DNA wouldn't have been a surprise. Our lab in Opelousas Parish isn't the fanciest, but it does the job. The only DNA they could find, other than Larry's, wasn't discovered until the samples were sent down here. The whole thing just feels a little too convenient."

"What does your sheriff think?"

"He doesn't like other jurisdictions doing his job for him, but once the killings stopped up north, he was happy to turn over the files."

"And yet you carry those drawings with you," Sere said, glad that the guy appeared to be working alone.

"I'm not looking to cause you problems, but I do want to hear what you know without all the bullshit. If I can save people's lives, I have an obligation to do so."

Noble. Stupid but noble. "The alligator hunters should stick to their established grounds," Sere said. "They have been warned."

"About what?"

The deputy was like a bloodhound who'd picked up a scent and couldn't think about anything else until he'd tracked down the source. Sere reconsidered her approach. *Maybe he could be of use up north. Lord knows I could use the help.*

"Fisher and I were involved in apprehending the Swamp Strangler. You can put your mind to rest regarding that case. But as you've apparently guessed, that monster wasn't alone. The serial killer's people are fiercely protective of their territory. If the gator hunters were poaching in the deep swamp, I'm surprised any of them got out alive." Sere's explanation was close enough to the truth that she didn't worry about the slight amount of fudging.

"And what happens if the gator hunters keep acting like children going out into the field to poke the hornet's nest?"

"What did the three survivors have to say about their nine dead companions?"

He casually opened one of the files. "This is where the story runs off the rails for me. I was able to interview them alone and individually, so the rest of the story is strictly between them, me, Ram, and now you. Each of them described a band of men running wild in the swamp like a pack of rabid dogs. What they described didn't even sound like *men*. Red eyes, sharpened teeth, and running on all fours—it was like they were describing some children's horror-story demon."

In spite of Deputy Thibodaux's dogged determination, he fortunately did not appear to believe in ghosts and goblins. "Other than describing a shared hallucination based on campfire horror stories," Sere asked, "did the men have anything useful to contribute to the myth?"

Evert Thibodaux gave Sere a tilted-head grimace of disbelief. "If they were delusions, having all three be identical would be one hell of a big coincidence—though it's not unusual up north for people hauled into the sheriff's office to spend some time getting their stories straight before being separated. One of the hunters did come up with a slight variation, claiming that the lead demon didn't have any skin, but he was pretty distraught after having seen his partner torn to shreds."

One more confirmed demon opening in life. Sere focused on her breathing, face muscles, and tone of voice in order to appear as calm as possible. "Have there been any other sightings of these creatures?"

The deputy leaned back in his chair. "That's exactly the

same look Ram gave me when he asked that question. What are you two hiding?"

Fuck! "We had a run-in with another mythical creature. The Swamp Strangler didn't appear altogether human."

"And since one swamp horror story crawled out of the bayou, you fear others will do the same?" he asked.

"Mythical monsters aside, one serial killer did find his way in from the swamp, and like I said, I believe he has kin out where no one can find them. In all likelihood, that's who your hunters ran across. In my experience, the families deep in the bayou and cut off from civilization have some strange rituals. There's no reason the Swamp Strangler's people won't follow his lead. We only caught him because he strayed too far from home."

Evert looked at his pile of folders. "That's not very comforting."

You're telling me, she thought. Evert was more insightful than Sere had realized, but she still couldn't tell him that killing men for the fun of it wouldn't be the demon's primary goal.

"What happened with the dead men's boats?"

"That's another thing," he said. "When the hunters went out to retrieve them, they weren't there."

"Please tell me the hunters just rely on their lifetime in the swamp to figure out where they are and how to get back into town."

The deputy shook his head. "Would anyone be that stupid? In addition to GPS, every hunter who's spent any time out there carries laminated maps so they can mark their trap locations with grease pencils."

"What you're telling me is those murderers now not only have transportation, but they also know where they're going. You might want to deputize anyone you think can responsibly carry a gun."

They had clearly passed beyond Lefty's ability to control the danger, although at least Bart hadn't sent his cousin down to New Orleans with tales of demons hitting shore. "Have you got any more good news for me?"

"That's about everything on the missing men." He pulled out another file from his case. "Which just leaves this. There was a killing in Riley's bar earlier this week. As is frequently the case in bar brawls, no one got a clear look at the winner —not unexpected, since they were all inebriated. Riley is being as tight-lipped as ever about the fight. Again, not a surprise, as her customers would dry up if she started ratting them out. You wouldn't happen to know anything about it?"

Sere let out an unusually long breath of relief. She wasn't the target of another investigation—not yet, anyway. "Why ask me?"

"Like I said earlier, there have been rumors of your nightly motorcycle rides and the physical altercations that follow. But mostly, I'm giving you that copy as a favor to Ram. Are you two involved in some gory courtship ritual? Blood and guts turn you on? Because I can't for the life of me figure out why he'd want you to have copies of these coroner pictures."

Sere opened the file a little too fast. *Please don't show me this mothergänger regenerating.* After seeing the coroner's visual documentation of the decapitation, she closed her eyes and let out another tellingly long breath. "What happened to the body?"

"This shit really does do it for you, doesn't it? Good lord —you are one fucked-up chick. He was cremated just like every other unclaimed body. The sheriff is inclined to file this as just one more idiot who ended up in a fight with the wrong person in the wrong bar. Personally, I'd rather try to save the living than spend my time hunting down someone who had let their aggression get the better of them."

Sere got up from behind the desk. "You seem like a nice guy. My advice is you go back to arresting drunks and investigating whatever small-town dramas land on your desk."

The cop got out of his chair and nodded at the shotgun propped up in the corner. "Looks like you know how to take care of yourself. Bart hinted at your fighting skills. If things get squirrelly up in my neck of the woods, can I count on you to point me in the right direction?" His help apparently came with a price.

"I've pretty much told you what I can without going back out into the swamp. The people I've met up your way didn't take too kindly to me. Having me on your side might make it harder to get information out of the bikers and hunters. If Bart agrees that I'm needed, get word to our receptionist, and I'll do what I can. For now, however, I think I'm better off protecting the people of New Orleans."

SERE SPENT the rest of the day analyzing the pieces of the

police reports that the deputy had left out of the official version. Imagining the battle out in the swamp came all too easily for her. At first glance, the odds seemed to favor the human contingent, with four doppelgängers facing twelve armed hunters. That must have been what the hunters imagined as well. The idiots probably thought the small band of swamp dwellers were trying to keep the prize gators for themselves. They must have had quite the surprise when the alligators rose up in unison and joined their demonic swamp companions. She couldn't fault the alligators for doing what came naturally. As soon as a doppelgänger injured a human, the gator squad would instinctively move in for the kill.

For the love of humanity, I hope that's what happened. So long as it was the living creatures—not the demons from hell—who performed the killings, there wouldn't be another opening in life. She scoured the reports for any mention of a doppelgänger committing the actual murder. Other than the one account the deputy had mentioned, however, she couldn't find another instance of the demons finishing the job.

She reread the single account of the doppelgänger-on-human killing. "Once the demon brought Charlie down by taking a bite of his calf, an alligator moved in to devour the body, the same as with the others. But before the fifteen footer could move in for the kill, the demon started tearing at Charlie's neck. I can still hear him screaming. I shot my rifle as fast as I could recock it, but with the gator in the way, my bullets just bounced off the reptile's hide like I was throwing spit wads. When the gator finally got the hint, I managed to plug the demon in the chest."

The deputy had inserted a handwritten note. "PJ is visibly shaking. I'm giving him a break so he can get some water. Whatever he saw out there has clearly affected his mental state."

The narrative continued. "I can't explain it. Blood squirted out of the dude's chest from my bullet. I was certain he would fall to the ground. But the longer I watched, the more determined he became. It was like he healed out of sheer force of will. Then he ripped poor Charlie's head clear off his shoulders like he was searching for something inside the body. Next thing I knew, he was going after Pete. Something had changed, though. I could see every muscle, organ, and vein in the demon's body, as if it didn't have any skin at all. No matter how many times I plugged it full of lead, it just kept coming. I guess Pete was lucky that an alligator swept in for the kill. Sure beat what Charlie had to endure. That's when I got the fuck out of there. I'm telling you, Evert, I don't ever want to go out to that section of swamp again."

Sere closed the file and tossed it to the side. The encounter out in the deep swamp had been mayhem, but then, she *had* warned the hunters to stay clear. Nowhere in the accounting was there any mention of a human taking out a doppelgänger.

"I suppose I should be grateful the demons only killed one man. So now I've got four known doppelgängers to deal with and one potential opening. Guess I'll have to watch the skies a little more carefully tonight."

"Did you want something, dear?"

Linda's voice over the intercom made Sere swat aside the file she had so casually tossed on the call button. She cautiously touched the aged plastic as if it were going to bite her. "Sorry, Linda. I dropped something on the intercom."

"No problem, dear. Happens all the time."

I'll bet. That woman probably knows more about what goes on in this office than Fisher. Sere was no wiz with technology, but it wasn't hard to imagine the sweet, innocent-looking old woman opening the old plastic box and rigging the intercom to always transmit whatever was said in the office.

I'm letting my mistrust of people get the better of me. But really, how much would it cost to update his system? I've seen Fisher's computers. The man's no stranger to modern electronics. I'll bet anything Linda is the one manipulating him into sticking with this old system.

Linda poked her nose into the office as if she'd heard Sere's thoughts. "There isn't anything else you can do for Mr. Fisher tonight. You should go home and get some rest. You look like you haven't slept in days."

"You have no idea."

11

*S*ere dumped her saddlebags on the dusty armchair in her loft above the Scratchy Dog. It seemed like months since she'd snuck out the bathroom window. The two snakes slithered out of the alligator-skin bags and slunk up the wood beam to their usual resting place in the rafters.

"It's not home, but it's safe."

They rattled their tired agreement.

"I suppose we're all a little beat. Maybe Linda was right. I should try to get some rest." Without even kicking off her boots, she lay on the saggy mattress and listened to the latest of Kendell's band discoveries belting out numbers she couldn't identify. The music provided an anchor to reality.

Being so far from the latest hellmouth meant she didn't have to worry quite as much about demonic dreams. She still hated sleeping—there were too many alternate realities threatening to suck her in. Slipping into the unconscious

167

state reminded her of being a recently deceased seven-year-old girl in Guinee and being pulled into hell.

As Sere drifted, reality took on the hazy quality, indicating that sleep was only a few gentle breaths away. *One, two...*

The shock of being back in her father's bank office made Sere's heart literally stop beating. She grasped her chest, desperate to feel a pulse, but was distracted by her unlikely surroundings. *He can't have escaped the loas.*

She closed her eyes and focused on the unwilling organ like Myles trying to start the grumpy VW. "I'm not dying today. Come on, beat, damn it." A single pump of her heart gave her something to build on, then there was another. "One more and I'll let you be." The soft, rhythmic beat sounded infinitely better than the old bus's engine finally coming to life. She breathed a little easier. *Okay, so in this dream, I'm not immortal. Kind of sucks.*

With her life no longer at risk, she looked around the office. The only thing that had changed was the lack of a door. "So I'm trapped in here." The feeling wasn't all that different from any other time she'd been in the old heavily masculine office. Her father had a way of making anyone feel trapped in his presence. "But you're not here, are you, old devil?" She closed her eyes and tried to hear the music pounding downstairs, but all she got was silence.

"Sorry to keep you waiting."

I know that voice. Sere clenched her fists. "You!"

She opened her eyes and saw the loa of the seventh gate, Baron Samedi, sitting behind the heavy oak desk like a judge waiting to pass out sentencing. "Be grateful that it's only me and that we're meeting here and not at your grave."

"Grateful? Hell, you want to steal my spirit."

His all-black eyes bore into her like death itself staring longingly at her soul. "I don't have to steal what already belongs to me. You took your life. We accepted you into our realm."

"And my father redeemed me."

"*He* stole you." The loa's voice boomed around the room like thunder.

Sere made her customary scan of the room for tactical advantages and adversarial threats. *Long, heavy desk, useful for vaulting off of—I can hit any wall with one good jump or hand thrust. A large painting of my father, the old goat. The frame could be a useful weapon. Andirons next to the fireplace. It's just the two of us in this cage match, and that old fart looks like he'd snap like a matchstick.*

She eased back into the comparatively small leather chair meant to make any guest feel weak. *He's trying to outmaneuver me. If he meant to haul me back to Guinee, we wouldn't be having this conversation.*

"Did you really bring me here to debate who owns my soul?"

Baron Samedi settled back into the massive bank president's chair. "This interdimensional gate is neutral ground. Events are progressing over which we don't have control. I'm here to determine if you are strong enough to act as our champion."

Like I would ever fucking work for you assholes! She tried not to let her irritation get the better of her. "What if I'm not interested?"

"I think you will be, but first, I need to know that you're *human* enough to do what's needed."

What the hell does that mean? But before she could modify the thought, into a nonconfrontational question, the scene of the heavily paneled office dissolved into the front of a suburban tract home late at night. The red and blue strobe lights of a police cruiser lit up the neighborhood.

JENNIFER CRANSTON STOOD SHIVERING in the warm humid air. "What? I don't understand."

"You're just in shock, honey. Don't worry. I'm sure Bobby will be okay."

Unlike Sere's other ride alongs with Jennifer's soul, this time, there was no one else at the controls. *Fuck! What has that asshole of the dead done now? Jennifer must be stuck in the godforsaken office while I play out his twisted game. But is this real or just Samedi's idea of a test?*

"Ma'am?" The police officer had the worried look of someone about to call in a medical professional.

"I'm sorry. I'm okay. Just tell me again what happened to my son." A maternal instinct she didn't know existed replaced the boy's name with his relationship to her at the last moment.

"He got on the school bus, but no one saw him get off. That driver keeps very close tabs on his riders, so Bobby's disappearance isn't an oversight on his part. Is there any reason why your son would have snuck off at a different stop? Maybe to see one of his friends?"

Sounds reasonable, Sere thought, though her pounding heart argued that such a thing would never happen. "Bobby knows better than to do something so reckless."

The conflict between how Sere, the badass demon hunter, analyzed information and how Jennifer's motherly body retained the truth made her knees weak. She crumpled into Henry's arms.

"I need to get my wife inside," he said.

The police officer closed his notebook and stashed it in his shirt pocket. "Of course. Rest assured that we're on this. I know it's difficult, but try to get some rest. We'll call you the moment we know anything."

Sere had never experienced so much trouble making her body obey her commands. Her arms and legs felt like limp spaghetti noodles. Her stomach rolled round and round like a front-loading washing machine. If it weren't for her husband at her side, she doubted she could see clearly enough to navigate her way to the front door.

But he's not my husband. And Bobby isn't my son. The words in her mind seemed to come from far away, like a dream she still remembered but was waking out of. *No. This is not me—it's my real's life.* She shook her head against Henry's shoulder.

His arm around her waist was like an anchor chain of love, preventing her from drifting away into worry and grief. "I've got you. Bobby's a smart boy. He'll figure out a way of getting a message to us."

"He's eight years old. Eight, Henry. If he tries to escape,

they'll hurt him." Tears welled uncontrollably in her eyes and ran down her face.

"There's no point in jumping to conclusions. No one has said anything about him being kidnapped. All I meant was he knows we love him."

Henry's arms eased off of their firm hold. Gravity took over, directing her into the overstuffed couch cushions. *Why is this body so useless?*

"I'm going to fix us a couple of stiff drinks," he said as he stood.

"Do we have any Jameson's? I'd kill for two fingers straight up."

He smiled at her in the slightly confused, goofy way he did when she'd said something unexpected. "I'm sure I have a bottle around here somewhere for guests."

Once he was out of the room, she began her tactical assessment. *Body feels like it's been sedated, but that's probably just due to emotions. This dress is useless for going on the hunt. I'll need to change. My jogging outfit should work. But where would I even begin?* Her heart was beating uncontrollably. Her eyes produced so many tears that she wondered if dehydration would become an issue. Wrapping her arms around her stomach, she sought any rejuvenating energy within reach.

With no other spiritual help available, she accepted the tumbler of whiskey Henry handed her. "Thank you, dear."

He sat on the couch at her feet and pulled off her pumps. His hands performed their usual magic of calming her nerves by massaging her ankles and arches, while the alcohol warmed her stomach. "Do you really think he snuck off to see a friend? It's not like him to be out after dark. Maybe we should start calling everyone he knows."

Henry's hands worked up to the base of her calf. "We need to let the police do their job. If we tie up our phones they, or Bobby, won't be able to reach us."

He'd always been better than her in a crisis, even in high school. *I still can't believe I messed up that cheerleading tumble so badly. My fucking knee was clear out of the socket.* She looked down at him rubbing her leg. "Do you know when I first fell in love with you? It was that moment you jumped out of the stands, grabbed my leg almost like you're doing now, and firmly set it back in place. I didn't even know you except as the know-it-all in civics. I'd have fucked you that night if you'd asked. But like the gentleman you are, you never cashed in on that debt. No other boy I knew at the time would have had any qualms about taking advantage of me."

He eased back to her ankle. "You were the popular girl and had something of a reputation. You can't exactly blame them."

Cock-loving popular cheerleader. But I should be focused on Bobby. That poor boy must be so scared. She sat up out of Henry's grasp and took another shot of the whiskey. "I can't just sit here doing nothing. You stay by the phone. I'm going to change into my running outfit and take a walk down to the park."

She could see in his face how much he wanted to object, but if she truly wanted something, he always gave in eventually. The entire argument played out with only a couple of facial expressions. "Keep your cell phone on you," he finally said, "and check in every fifteen minutes. I mean it, Jen-Jen." He reserved the old pet name for times when he needed her cooperation but didn't want to fight about it.

She pulled the block of technology out of her purse. "I promise. Look, I'll set the timer app so I won't forget."

OUTSIDE, Jennifer-Sere felt more at ease alone in the dark. Neither mentally nor physically did she want to be cooped up with nothing to do while her child was in danger. As she rounded the corner leading into the park, her phone vibrated through the leather purse pressed against her hip. *This should be interesting.*

Her hand reached into her bag as if on autopilot, pressed a thumb to the button to unlock it, and called Henry. "I'm just getting to the park now. Any word?"

"Nothing yet." Hearing the words come through on the digital speaker made her ear cringe. *Is that due to what he just said, or am I experiencing a cell phone for the first time?*

"It's only been fifteen minutes," she said into the rectangular block of plastic. "I guess we can't expect an immediate update. I'm going to wander down along the river. You know how much he likes to fish. Call you in fifteen."

"Love you. Please be safe." Even the casual sign of affection made her heart flutter.

"I promise." The funny thing was, Sere really believed what she was saying.

After resetting the timer and stashing the phone back among the compacts and crumbled receipts, she headed for the highest knoll in the rolling green space. *I wish I had my snakes with me.* A quivering deep in her gut let Sere know that Jennifer was not benevolently inclined toward the slithery little monsters.

Sere's first inclination was to look for threats, ambush sites, and places where she could set up to best observe the goings-on below, but Jennifer took a mother's angle on the problem. "Where would a frightened eight-year-old boy go to hide?"

The stomach-wrenching fear matched up with a memory from just after Henry had moved their family out of the big city. Jennifer had taken a much younger Bobby to this same park to explore. He'd gotten away from her. The memory of those quivering, heart-palpitating few minutes had prevented her from ever returning to the park with her son.

But where did he go? Sere tried to access Jennifer's memories but came up with nothing. Though she scanned the playground, open field, and dog park, nothing struck her as familiar. Bobby had simply reappeared at his mother's side.

Clever little fellow, aren't you? Sere got down on her knees to see the terrain from Bobby's perspective. *Rolling down the grassy hill would be a blast. Looking for bugs and worms would be cool too.* The babbling riffle in the river called to her like a playmate splashing in the stream, but she didn't know if that was because of her swamp upbringing or Jennifer's motherly empathy.

Unlike Jennifer, having been raised in the wild made Sere gravitate to nature's call. *There's no harm in checking.*

What are you waiting for? Sere combated the motherly instinct to rush down to the water. Instead, she lay flat on her stomach to read the ankle-tall grass. *If this is something more than a boy getting lost, I need to know what I'm walking into.*

The lights from the road left pockets of shadows where the terrain rose and fell toward the water. Regularly spaced hop prints told of a rabbit casually traversing the open plain. The bunny trail took on an urgency just as a pair of child's sneaker-toe prints rounded down from the road.

He never could resist something soft and fuzzy. A memory based on the emotions of Bobby opening his Christmas present only to have the kitten jump out and run along his arms threatened to get the best of Sere. *Stop showing me how much you love your kid. I've got work to do.* She got off her knees and crept along the crushed-grass trail. *If this path is from Bobby, at least I don't see any demon tracks following him.*

Demon? The word echoed around her gut like a two-week-old chicken casserole, but she didn't have time to dwell on the hidden dangers that worried her the most. *One rescue at a time.*

She slipped off her running shoes and ankle socks to walk barefoot through the grass. Every few feet, she checked the path to be sure no other creature had snuck in behind the boy chasing the rabbit.

At the water's edge, her razor-sharp mom hearing picked up the plaintive repeated cry of "Mommy."

"Bobby? Is that you?" Her heart pounded so hard she could barely hear the boy's crying.

Slowly. It could be a trap.

But Jennifer's legs weren't paying attention to reason. She jumped into the swiftly moving stream and started yelling her son's name while searching every hollow in the riverbank.

Bobby sat huddled under the outstretched protective oak-tree roots that projected from the riverbank. His skinned arms were tightly wrapped around the torn legs of his school uniform pants. Rocking back and forth while quietly sobbing, he apparently hadn't heard Jennifer's initial call. He sure as hell heard her scream of joy, though.

"Mommy!" He nearly fell face-first into the water as he jumped to his feet.

Sere bent down and caught him in midstride. Hugging him so tightly she feared she might hurt his ribs, she hoisted him off his feet. "Oh my God! I was so worried about you. Are you okay?" Part of her wanted to hold Bobby out so she could inspect his bruises, but the more powerful instinct of not letting him go won out.

"I hurt my arm."

She noticed he only had one arm around her neck while the other hung limply at his side. "It's okay, baby. Let me have a look." Tenderly, she set him back on the shore and ran her hand up from his wrist. *He's moving his fingers, so there shouldn't be anything broken.* The way the whole arm turned in her hands made her quicken her inspection of his shoulder. *Dislocated.* "I need you to be really brave for just a minute. You've already been such a big boy." Before he had a chance for fear to set in, she gripped his arm and wrist. With one quick tug and twist, she had it back in the socket.

"Owie!" he screamed through his cries.

She desperately wanted to return him to her chest to hug the pain and fear out of him, but where there was one injury, there were bound to be more. "Tell Mommy where else it hurts."

He pulled at the tattered edge of his ripped pants. A two-inch gash was seeping blood. *It's not squirting—that's good—but he's been out here a couple of hours, so who knows how much blood he's lost.*

She looked around in part to see if there was anyone close by who could help but also to make sure she wasn't seen. "I want you to close your eyes, my love. This isn't going to hurt. Mommy is going to do a little Mommy magic, okay?"

He nodded and put his hands up to his eyes.

All right, you fucking loa. Make this work, or suffer my wrath. She squeezed her well-manicured fingernails into the palm of her hand until blood oozed down to her wrist. Then she pressed the open wound to Bobby's leg. *If I could only transfer spiritual energy without that damn paranormal bandage.*

An aura of confusion made Sere squeeze her eyes closed as she gripped the boy's leg. Blood from both wounds stopped flowing. When she took her hand away, she ran her fingers over her palm. *Not perfect, but good enough.*

She bent down and cradled Bobby in her arms. "What do you say we go home, kiddo?"

His soft blond hair tickled her cheek as he nodded.

"What happened?" She nearly hated asking, but if there was a threat at hand, she needed to know about it before she carried him unprotected across an open field.

"I'm so sorry. I didn't mean to get lost." His words trailed off into a prolonged sob.

"I'm not mad at you, sweetheart. I'm just so happy I found you. I was so worried."

He grabbed her around the neck so hard that if it had been a battle, she'd have had to throw him off before he cut off her circulation. "I saw a bunny hopping through the grass. A man was hiding behind a tree with a gun. He was going to shoot it." Again, Bobby's voice was reduced to incomprehensible sobs.

Sere put her hand on the boy's head so she could peer over his shoulder. The rabbit tracks he had followed disappeared over the tree roots. Bobby must have lost his footing and fallen into the river. Rabbits, however, were typically a little more surefooted than eight-year-old boys. The animal's prints stopped at the roots' highest point. Sere slowly turned while scanning the water and the opposite muddy riverbank. A man's bare footprint stood out plain as day across the river, in line with where the rabbit had jumped.

She pressed her hand to Bobby's ear and cradled him against her cheek. The shades of blue, gray, and dark green of the small ravine took on a tinge of red. *If any of you doppelfuckwads lays one grimy finger on this precious boy, I'll travel back to hell and cut off every demon's head I come to.*

Sere held the boy even tighter as she felt her spirit being ripped from the mother's body.

SERE DIDN'T REALLY CARE if Baron Samedi was more spirit than physical. She leapt up from the office chair, gripped it by the armrests, and flung it over the desk at the bank president's opulent throne. "What the hell was that about?" she screamed as the two pieces of furniture splintered on impact.

The loa of the dead stood up from the tangled mass of wood and cushions that had passed right through him. "I had to know how you would face the threat to a loved one."

"I'd fucking bash the villain's face in. That's how." She longed for a good drag-down knockout fight over whatever game the baron was playing.

"Fortunately for everyone, your actions proved otherwise." He picked up his top hat and cane. "Not every battle can be won single-handedly, Sere Mal-Laurette. Sometimes a warrior's strongest move isn't violence."

As the baron dissolved into nothingness, so did the room. She woke out of the spiritual nightmare covered in sweat. "What the hell was that supposed to prove? At least the fucker didn't take my soul." Her defiance, however, was tempered by a longing to make sure both Bobby and Jennifer were all right.

Professor Yates might be brilliant enough to create an alternate reality like the one she'd just experienced, but she'd never heard of the loas doing anything other than pass judgment on people's souls. She needed to find out if the previous night's adventure had been real or imagined. *And if it was real, poor Jennifer. That woman must still be terrified. I'll bet Bobby doesn't breathe fresh air for a week.*

12

*A*fter Sere stashed her motorcycle in its hiding spot for the day, she grabbed her saddlebags and headed for the office. "Linda, do you think you could find me a newspaper?" She tried to make the request not sound too insane. *Only two days at the job, and the receptionist already must think I'm bonkers.*

"Of course, dear, but most people find what they want online. I can get a computer out of storage if you'd like. The building has Wi-Fi, but it's been a little glitchy lately."

I'll bet it has. "Just a good old-fashioned newspaper would be great. Something that still reports the activities of the last twenty-four hours."

The old woman scrunched up her face. "I am familiar with the concept."

Sere didn't admit that newspapers were new to her. She'd spent most of her life in hell, where the previous day's tortures were not reported. "Any word on Mr. Fisher?"

Linda's face brightened. "He's in his office."

And all is right with your world. "Think it'd be okay if I poke my nose in?"

"I'm sure he's expecting you, hon."

Before heading into the main office, Sere unlocked her private sanctuary and dropped off her bags. A box of shotgun shells lay open on the desk, but only a handful were missing. At least Fisher had planned ahead, but then, he was probably better at anticipating what was to come than Sere was.

She knocked softly on Fisher's open solid-wood door. "You busy?"

He leaned back from his desk, which was covered in spreadsheets. "I've always got time for you, my dear." The kindly CPA had regained his welcoming smile and sparkling eyes. Only the bandage wrapped around his head indicated that not everything was hunky-dory.

Sere closed the door behind her and took a seat. "What the hell was that adventure about? You could have gotten yourself killed. If you even think about going off on a mission again without telling me, you'll find one of my snakes tagging along in your briefcase."

He raised his palms at her as if she were physically attacking him. "Easy, Demon Huntress. I'd hoped that I could reason with Thomas, possessed to possessed, but he's farther gone into the darkness than I expected. I figured he'd be fighting against his demon just as I was. On that count, I was mistaken."

After her night of saving a young boy from his noble, if foolish, desire to play the hero, she didn't have it in her to harangue a grown man for a similar misadventure. "What else did you learn?"

"He's being manipulated, though by whom and from where, I can't say."

She stared into Fisher's eyes, looking for any hint of red. "You told him you were hearing the same voice in your dreams."

"It's true. I didn't want to worry you about it until I had a little more information. Dreams aren't real, after all, and my nightly tossing and turning could have just been from my late-night mocha-almond-fudge ice cream obsession."

Sere almost told him about her own disturbing dreams of the previous night, but she didn't want to add to Fisher's concerns for her. "What is the voice telling you to do?"

"'Prepare the way.' It's just the same three words repeated like a broken soundtrack over my dreams. Typically, my sleep is filled with stories about life in the Quarter or being at home—not very creative, I know. Lately, the dreams start out that way, but then they transition into some kind of post-apocalypse nightmare. That's usually when I wake up."

Lucky you.

"Any idea what the words mean?" Sere had her suspicions, of course, but Fisher was the one tuned into hell's mouth.

"That's what I was hoping to find out from Thomas. I should have known he'd try to escape."

She picked up one of the three shotgun shells from his desk. "And what made you force-feed him a paranormal pellet?"

He blushed like a kid who'd just been busted for raiding the cookie jar. "Sorry about the petty theft. I have images of you and that hunky military dude saving my life. Though at the time I was being consumed by my demon and in a state of shock, some memories remain crystal clear. You were in a panic when you screamed at that commando to shoot my doppelgänger. A part of me still recoils when I'm in the same room as those shells. I figured if I had such a strong reaction to them, Thomas would as well. It wasn't like I had a lot of options for how to confront him. Speaking of which, I could use a weapon. I can't wander the French Quarter with nothing more than a letter opener. If the doppelgängers are going to come after me like alligators after a wounded chicken, I need to be able to defend myself."

Sere couldn't imagine the nice man having much in the way of fighting skills. "Whoever is behind these escapes from hell doesn't have his sights on you."

"Maybe not, but those demons see me as a traitor to their cause. You're not the only one at risk."

He was right about that. Sere asked, "Have you ever fired a gun?"

"My sweet naïve superhero, I'm a southern boy. I learned to shoot before I learned to drive. Ann made me get rid of my firearms when our first daughter was born. She said she didn't want Kristine to grow up in a world where her parents felt it necessary to be forever on guard. I used to keep a rifle in the office in case I got a particularly belligerent client. When people learn that the IRS is after them, not everyone takes it sitting down. Some of my customers act like they've just found out the devil's on their tail and decide the best course of action is to kill the messenger. But somehow, Linda managed to store the rifle where I can't find it." He leaned over the desk conspiratorially. "I suspect she's in cahoots with my wife."

Sere leaned forward as well. "Can you blame them?"

"Hey, now. Before I met you, I lived a very respectable life—father, husband, and upstanding member of the business community."

"Before you met me, you were practically a hobbit."

His laugh had a way of easing her heart's worries. "Maybe so. Being the sidekick to a superhero does have its moments. Not that anyone would believe the stories even if I could tell them."

He did need protection. If Sere thought they could handle it, she would give everyone she knew a box of supernatural shotgun shells. "I've got a single-barrel blaster in my office as backup. You can use that. I'll throw in a box of hell's shells and a box of paranormal half loads. After your run-in with Thomas, it seemed prudent to prepare some ammunition that would equally affect the living and the demonic."

A COPY of the *Times Picayune* lay open on Sere's desk. She sat back in her chair, feeling like a real businesswoman, as she opened the paper. The story she both searched for and dreaded was on page three: "Mother Finds Lost Child in Jackson Park."

"Fuck." Sere looked across her desk to make sure she hadn't once again depressed the intercom button by mistake. Then she laid the paper flat on the desk and began reading.

"Mrs. Jennifer Cranston of Kenner first heard of her missing son at 9:00 p.m. last night when she returned home to find a police cruiser parked in front of her house. The boy had been reported missing by the school authorities after the bus he was riding in returned to the yard without a record of him disembarking. In a state of panic, Mrs. Cranston ran from her house, yelling for her son."

Sensationalist, irresponsible bullshit reporting. Sere read on, trying not to let her disgust with the news profession get the better of her.

"Her motherly instinct paid off. Bobby Cranston had snuck out of the bus on a whim and nearly drowned while playing hooky."

He wasn't playing hooky, and he didn't almost drown, you asswipe reporter.

"Mrs. Cranston was still in a state of shock when this reporter was finally able to get a few words. 'I never understood what people meant about having an *out-of-body experience.* I sure do now. It was like I was watching my actions from some observation room. I didn't even know I had that level of bravery in me. I guess it's true—a mother's love can make a woman do all kinds of things she didn't think were possible.'"

Sere folded the paper and stashed it in the bottom drawer of the desk. *It was fucking real. Goddamn that loa asshole.* But of greater concern than the dream's basis in reality was whatever had tempted Bobby off the bus. A guy with a gun who ran off and a rabbit that transformed into a man... these were not normal occurrences. Either the loas or the damned had tricked Bobby.

But maybe it had just been to test her. Sere felt the familiar raised hair on the back of the neck that told her she was missing something important.

13

---

*E*ach time the brittle speaker on Sere's desk crackled to life, she cringed. *At least Linda is toying with the button first instead of making me jump out of my skin.*

"Miss Sere, there's a man here to see you. He doesn't have an appointment."

One of your cardinal sins, Sere thought. Having the receptionist ask his name or get any pertinent information would just drag out the inevitable meeting. "Go ahead and send him in."

The bartender of Bubba's Bar and Grill filled the small doorway with his broad shoulders. "Rampart Thibodaux." He extended his hand as if this were their first meeting. Sere wasn't sure if Bart was just being overly obnoxious or if he thought he was saving her from the nosy receptionist's prying questions.

She shook his hand, unsure of what else to do. "That's a mouthful."

His dreamy-eyed smile and raised eyebrow made her realize she'd stepped into a double-entendre trap. "You have no idea."

She wasn't about to let him get the upper hand so easily. She let her gaze fall from his eyes to directly on the bulge in his tight leather riding pants. "I don't know about that. You don't leave much to a woman's imagination."

He wasn't coy in allowing himself the same visual caress along her body. In any case, he already knew what she looked like naked. "Fortunately for me, I have a remarkably good memory," he said.

Sere knew when she was outmatched in terms of sexual innuendo. She stood aside so he could enter and get out of Linda's not-so-subtle inspection of his backside. *Dirty old woman—though I can hardly blame you.*

Sere turned her attention back to Bart. "So you've finally decided saving the world is more important than popping open beer bottles for a bunch of lazy drunks?" she asked as she shut the door.

He sat in the guest chair and kicked his leather boots up onto her desk. "Not the whole world—just your scrawny ass."

There it is. Now we're back to the snarky banter. She sat behind her desk like the professional she was supposed to be. "I'm fully aware that I'm in hell's crosshairs. Tell me something I don't know."

He stretched out on the chair and clasped his hands behind his head as if he owned the place. "I had four new customers at the bar last night. Those demons hold their alcohol about as well as freshman girls at a frat party. From their loud conversations, I gathered it's not really you they're after." In spite of his casual stance, the even tone of his voice conveyed the grave importance of his words, even though she missed his point.

"Come again?"

"Actually, I guess it is the *real* you. I overheard them talking about Jennifer Ellen—"

"Fucking Cranston!" The colors in Sere's office faded to shades of red. "So that's what those assgängers are up to." She looked at Bart out of the corner of her eye. "How did you know about my connection to Jennifer?"

"You did tell me you were a doppelgänger. That meant you had to have a real person around here somewhere."

Though it involved trusting Bart with even more personal information, she couldn't let the half-truth stand. *I need him to know.* "Only my body is doppelgänger. Unlike these demonic marionettes from hell, I have a soul as well."

He stared at her as if she'd just opened her shirt and flashed him her breasts. "Sounds like an intriguing story for another time. When those demonic idiots kept fixating on the same person, it wasn't hard to figure out the connection. After all, who's a bigger threat to them than you? But just to make sure, I stopped by Joe's cabin on my way down here. From the worried look he failed to hide, I knew this was important."

"So they want to kill Jennifer," Sere said.

She really wished it was Joe sitting across the desk, delivering the bad news, but he was probably doing his thing behind the scenes. But the ramifications, though bad, weren't as disastrous as Bart might think. Professor Yates had already indicated that he had enough data on the woman to keep Sere going indefinitely, even if her physical options might be a bit limited. *I would be free of her, but healing would take a lot longer.* Though the logical and tactical assessment eased Sere's personal worries, she couldn't shake the look in Bobby's big brown eyes when he saw her running to his rescue. *I can't have that boy grow up without a mother because of me.*

"I never heard the word kill," Bart said, interrupting her thoughts. "They just wanted to find her."

Shit. Having demons abduct Jennifer could be worse than having them kill her.

"What did Joe say when you told him what you'd heard?" she asked.

"To get my ass down here as soon as possible. Mind telling me why this woman is in so much danger?"

"Because she's an idiot." Sere's assessment was based less on emotion than practicality. "When I told Fisher that he had a double that was out to kill him, the man took the information in stride. We were able to formulate a plan, no thanks to your interference." She could tell from Bart's tensed muscles he was about to debate her conclusion so she hurried on without giving him an opening. "If we tell Jennifer someone's out to harm her, the woman will go running to the cops or tell her husband and end up in the insane asylum or do some other dumb-ass move I can't anticipate. She's like a little bunny. Tell her the big bad wolf is after her, and she'll hop around screaming the news to everyone she sees."

Bart unclasped his hands from behind his head and

rubbed the Navy SEAL tattoo on his arm, a sure sign that his military training was kicking in—Joe had the same unconscious tic when stressed. "So we have to covertly protect her. Anything else I need to know?"

Sere wondered how long it would be before she divulged all of her personal secrets. *Fuck it. I have to trust someone.*

"I can't be in the same place with her," she said. "The dangers to both of us aren't fully known, but they're bad."

With his feet still on her desk, he rocked the chair back and forth on its back legs. "I was there when you decapitated Monty. I saw what it did to Fisher. So that's the challenge: protect your real without her knowing about it. What are our resources?"

His confidence, though naïve, gave her a little spark of hope, but she couldn't put him in direct danger. Plus, he knew enough about her already and didn't need to poke around the woman who gave her substance just to gain information. Since she looked like Sere, he would probably flirt with her out of habit, and Jennifer was just cock hungry enough to fall for him.

"You seem to think this is a *we* operation."

He bent his knees as if about to bolt for the door and dropped the chair's front feet to the floor with a loud crash. "This is not the time for you to pull your *I can do it on my own* attitude. Tell me to leave, and I'm gone."

She needed help, and there weren't many who had the skill set to face combat. "I'm sorry. You're right." The words nearly made her choke, but she got them out.

The harsh lines around his deep-set brown eyes

softened. "I'm on your side, Sere. You don't have to push everyone who cares about you away."

Now you're sounding like Baron Samedi.

"Just don't try to take the lead," she said. "You don't know what we're facing."

"Fair enough, so long as you realize that my military skills surpass yours. That's not a cut against Joe's training. Honestly, that man has experienced more combat than I ever will. But what you know is based on computer simulations, one-on-one training, and fooling around in the swamp like a river otter. My skills have been forged in battle. That's not something that can be replicated."

The long-winded defense of his abilities almost made her smile. *He's trying so hard to convince me of his value.*

"This may come as a surprise, but I never doubted your abilities." She resisted the temptation to compare him to Joe. Other than that aging commando, she couldn't think of anyone she'd rather have on her side, but Bart didn't need any more of an ego boost. "Have you had any update from the bikers or hunters?"

Please tell me your bar was those demonic fuckers' first stop.

"You mean in the twenty-four hours since my cousin stopped by?"

She couldn't believe it had only been a day since the cop had introduced himself. "Things happen fast with those demons, in case you've forgotten," she said.

"You're not wrong there." He finally put his feet on the floor and leaned over the desk, looking ready to get to work. "According to the questionable information exchange, yesterday was a fucking bloodbath in the swamp.

I was hoping to enlist Joe to come down here so I could confirm the swamp rumors, but he said I was better off seeing you in person."

Fuck you, Joe. Paramilitary matchmaking meddler.

Bart continued on, not being privy to her inner tirade. "I didn't want to show up with gossip, but it sounds like only half of the hunters made it back to the dock last night. Whether the others encountered some mysterious boogeymen, got eaten by revenge-seeking gators, or simply drifted off toward the deep swamp to see things for themselves is anyone's guess. Riley's is closed out of respect for the dead. First time that's ever happened."

"That explains why the demons hit your bar instead of Riley's. Is there any way you could prevail on your cousin to find out what really happened out there?"

Bart gave her the same laser-sharp stare Joe used when he knew Sere was leaving out some vital bit of information. "Why?"

Do they teach you guys that stare in the military or something? Jeez. "Like your rumor," she said, "it's not a threat that I have well identified at this point. Until I do, I'd rather keep it to myself, but any demon-on-human killing might be important to know about."

He sat upright like a military commander awaiting orders. "So where do we start?"

The man wasn't all talk. Sere felt instantly gratefully. "If the demons are clear of the swamp, they'll be headed this way as quickly as possible. Since you met the doppelgängers at your bar and Joe hasn't checked in, I have to believe they're somewhere between the two locations. I'm going after them. I'm done playing defense. I just hope I'm not too late."

"You don't think they just took the boats back out to the swamp? It'd be a whole lot easier to escape detection out on the water."

"I don't for two reasons. First, we're talking serial killers here, not a military strike force. They'll be looking to create as much carnage as possible on their way to the city. And second, each of those demons' reals would be city folk. Their natural inclination will be to look at those maps to parallel the closest roads. Even in their boats, they'll stay close to shore."

He got out of the chair and hitched his tight leather pants up snug to his hips, making the bulge in the middle all the more prominent. "I'm going with you."

Part of her wanted to protect the big brute, but the tactician in her knew he was her best bet in a fight. *Fuck it. My track record against these demons on my own isn't the best.*

"I'd appreciate the company," she said.

"What do you want to do about Jennifer? You must have someone down here who can play babysitter?"

Sere grabbed the single-barrel shotgun from the corner of her office. "Fisher is about as kindly and nonthreatening a person as I've met. Plus, he has the ability to detect the demons when they're present, and he's more than proven his bravery."

Ann's going to kill me.

Bart responded slowly. She could practically see the wheels turning in his head. "I thought you didn't trust

Jennifer with the truth. Even with that scattergun, Fisher's not going to be a match for four demons."

"I'll tell him to keep his distance. This gun will just be for protection. If the demons get past us, then he can approach Jennifer. Between Kendell, her crew, and the homeless population in New Orleans, Jennifer should be safe until one of us reaches her."

Assuming the demons haven't killed us both.

"That secures our asset and gives us our hunting grounds," Bart said. "Where does Joe fit in?"

She wondered if the question was strategic or personal. *You want us to face this danger together—just the two of us? That might be the most romantic innuendo you've made to me.*

"He has hidden caches all along the swamp highway," she said. "Many of them double as backup command centers. He can provide coordination and, if need be, a first line of defense should we fail."

As she holstered her four-barrel shotgun, Bart checked his weapons. "Guess it's time to ride. You do remember our agreement?"

"When it comes to military action," she said, "you're in charge."

14

Out on the freeway, Sere—on her Triton café racer—settled in behind Bart's Ducati Monster. Though following was never her preferred position, even at full throttle, her little motorcycle was no match for the high-performance beast. *This isn't a race.* She consoled her slightly bruised ego by staring at his muscular ass. Like a poker player's tell, he broadcast every movement of the bike by first flexing the corresponding butt cheek.

By the time they'd left the crowded freeway for the rural highway, she had each of his motorcycle moves figured out. On a long, gentle curve, she cut tight inside his line and gave her little Triton all it could handle. Her smaller, lighter bike shot past his larger one like a fighter jet buzzing a cargo plane. The sound of his Ducati revving up in frustration was music to her ears. *Let's see how you like following my ass for a change.*

The game of motorcycle superiority kept Sere from

obsessing about the demons that lay ahead, but when she swung her bike onto the dirt road leading to Joe's cabin, she realized she should have stayed focused on the mission. A set of BSA tire tracks cut through the dust straight at her like a warning signal. She veered off the road into the grassy field and waved at Bart to follow.

He pulled up beside her and yanked off his black helmet. "What the hell?"

She nodded toward the road. "Those tracks are from Joe's motorcycle. Something's wrong."

"Maybe he just went out to get some smokes."

Sere got off her bike and crept toward the road to avoid disturbing the evidence. "Joe doesn't smoke."

"You know what I mean." Bart got off, too, but stayed behind her.

She pointed at the deep groove the bike had made when hitting a right-hand turn at high speed. "He's not that reckless. Either someone was chasing him, or he was in pursuit."

Bart tossed his helmet onto the seat of his bike and pulled the gun from the back of his pants. "Only one way to find out."

She pulled her shotgun and checked the chambered shells. *Two half-and-half loads and two full paranormal rounds.* "Joe's cabin is practically my second home. You take the road approach, and I'll sneak around from the back. If you see anyone but Joe, don't hesitate to shoot. You won't get many chances. That peashooter of yours will only slow a demon down. You're going to need one of those lovely knives of yours to finish it off."

He patted the Buck knife at his hip. "You don't have to remind me. Seeing you cut Monty's head off isn't something I'm likely to forget. I'll work my way along the opposite side of the road and take a position across from the front door. Once I hear you enter the cabin, I'll make my assault."

ONCE BART WAS SAFELY across the road, Sere started investigating the grass field. *No tracks. Not even a snake on patrol. I wonder what Joe would have to say about that.*

Instead of taking the direct path toward the cabin, she used the trees for cover and angled down to the river. If there had been a battle, the demons would have used a water approach, and Joe would have disabled every boat he could.

Nothing. Not even a muddy boot print. If they came this way, they were trying to surprise him. Something must have provoked Joe, though, or he would have gotten word to me that the demons had crossed his path before trying to engage them.

She snuck up under the raised deck that projected from the cabin out over the river. The pine-needle-covered yard beside the building looked messy, as though someone had been rolling around in the dirt. *They never made it into your house.* She got down on her knees to read the signs of battle.

Before she could get close to the first body-sized imprint, a hand gripped her hair and yanked her head back hard. Not leaving her time to react, a knife slashed across her throat. *How could I be so stupid?* She only hoped that wouldn't be her final thought.

A gunshot from the corner of the house hit her shoulder, corkscrewing her away from the blade as it came in for a second pass. The momentum ripped her hair out of assailant's hand. Instinctively, she grasped her neck to stem the bleeding and grabbed her knife out of her boot to counterattack.

The demon came at her from the front, slashing at her throat, but armed and ready this time, she drove her blade straight up under his chin, catching the edge of his knife on her forearm. His sharp edge cut through her muscles clear to the bone.

"You're not going to win," she rasped past the cut to her throat. She needed to keep pressing her advantage. Sere extended her damaged arm to shove her combat knife through the roof of his mouth and as deep into his brain as she could go. *That still won't kill him.*

The thick curved blade of Bart's Buck knife, coated in blood, cleaved through the demon's neck, leaving it impaled on Sere's knife like a candy apple on a stick.

As the doppelgänger's body crumpled to the ground, she saw Bart standing behind it, sweaty and blood splattered. The muscular bartender yanked off his riding jacket and ripped his shirt to ribbons like a shifter about to change into his animal double. "Don't panic. I've got you." He grasped her hand and pulled it away from her throat while wrapping the strips of his shirt around the wound. "I need to get you into the cabin. Joe has a med kit for you in the bedroom."

I'll bet he told you all of his secret locations. Fucker wouldn't even tell me, but he tells you? The anger energized her enough to accept Bart's arms around her body. Blood from her arm and shoulder soaked into the bustier. *I am not going to die.*

He jostled her in his arms as he ran for the front door. "You're losing a lot of blood. Even with what Joe told me about your anatomy, we're going to have to get you stable before hooking you up to Jennifer."

She tried to focus on what he was saying, but forming a response would have been beyond her mental ability even if she'd been able vocalize it past her severed larynx. He laid her on the bed before pulling out the steamer trunk from underneath. She reached for the technology-laced bandage that he'd so casually tossed beside her. *Dummy. That's what you wrap around my neck. What do you think you're doing?*

He stood up with a section of plastic hose wrapped tightly around his bicep. "Fortunately for you, I'm a universal blood donor."

You're a universal idiot, she wanted to say, but all that came out of her throat was a gurgling sound.

With his knife, he cut a notch in his arm then pushed another section of tubing into the incision. He fed the other end into the open gash on her forearm. With enough bandage to wrap a mummy, he finally stopped the blood that was rushing out of her like a river's open spillway.

"With all the blood that you've lost, it shouldn't be too hard for me to pump you back up." He flexed his arm hard, forcing the thick red liquid into her.

She couldn't turn away from his face. Between his lifeblood being forced into her, his heaving muscles, and most of all, his intense look of satisfaction, she could well imagine what he looked like during sex. *You're enjoying saving my life far too much.* Her heart returned to its normal beat as blood again filled the arteries.

He kept pumping while looking into her eyes. "There's the angry glare I've been waiting for. How about we give this technology stuff a go?" Without leaning over and disrupting the flow of blood, he pulled the connecting wires out from the trunk. "I know you can't talk, and I can't risk you deepening that cut along your neck by you moving your head, so just blink once for yes and two for no." He held up the wires. "The bandage at your throat is wrapped on top of my shirt. I don't want to undo it as you'll start bleeding out again, and I don't know how long you need to be connected to heal. Can I leave the cloth the way it is and just plug you in?"

How the hell am I supposed to know? She blinked once. Anything beat not being able to tell him off. At the very least, her arm would heal so she could punch him in the gut.

"Right. Joe said his computer communicates over old telephone cables down to New Orleans. I need to run these wires to the next room. Just lie still for a moment."

SERE DIDN'T EVEN GET a second to adjust to being inside Jennifer's body. The woman was completely out of breath. Her legs were pumping like she was sprinting the final leg of a marathon. Stumbling on the uneven terrain in the dark, she kept turning her head as if unsure of where to go.

"Why are you chasing me?" Jennifer screamed.

Shit. I'm too late to stop those fucking demons, Sere thought.

Look around, woman. I need to make my assessment. But Jennifer just kept running like some dimwit in a cheesy horror story. *How am I supposed to help you if I don't know for sure who you're running from?*

Nothing Sere thought seemed to matter. *Fuck Professor Yates and his equipment!* The check valves were doing their job of ensuring that Sere siphoned off the energy she needed without taking over the woman's life.

"Jennifer, stop," a voice yelled from behind her. "We're trying to help you."

That sounds like Joe. For the love of God, woman, let me get a look at what's going on around you.

Jennifer turned at the waist to see if her pursuer was gaining on her. The movement wasted a great deal of her momentum. *Joe! That's Joe, you fool. He's here to help you. Just stop. You're going to be okay.*

Even with the not-so-quick look behind her, Sere was able to make out the man in a white seersucker suit far behind the dude dressed in black military garb chasing Jennifer. Of course, Fisher would be trying to help. *Damn it, you're not in danger.*

But Sere's assessment of Jennifer's safety was only based on who was following her. The woman wasn't paying attention to where she was going and tripped over the same tree root Bobby had used as protection. Instead of splashing into the river, however, she tumbled into the swamp boat.

The sound of the outboard firing up drowned out the yelling of the men trying to save her. She edged toward the front of the boat to get as far away as possible from the men in pursuit.

"Thank you so much. I don't know what's going on. Can you take me to the police?" She looked up at the faces of the three men in the boat. Each had blood flowing from knife wounds to their faces and necks. Jennifer screamed so loudly that Sere felt as if she were being expelled from the woman's mouth.

SERE OPENED her eyes to see Bart sitting, covered in blood and half-naked, on the bed next to her with the wires in his hand. "You were screaming. That didn't seem like the best idea with that cut around your throat."

She put her hand to her neck and carefully moved her head from side to side. The wound had healed, but from just the gentle movement, she could tell talking wasn't going to be much fun. "They have her."

He dropped the cables and helped her up to the sitting position. "What did you see?"

"The fool fell right into their boat." Sere said, though she was in no position to judge. After all, she had just run straight into the doppelgängers' trap herself.

He unwrapped the cloth from her arm and eased the transfusion tube out of the sealed gash. "You're still in rough shape, but at least the flesh has closed up."

She pointed at his muscular arm with the tube still in place. "Why?"

He held up the line, which was still coated red on the inside. "When Joe was teaching me about your situation, he was very clear on one point: if you were facing immediate death, you would be too weak for the psychic link. You'd have to heal the slow way, and right now, we don't have that kind of time. I took a calculated risk."

She was still too weak to stand, and between Bart's blood and Jennifer's energy, she was a little mentally wobbly as well. "What happened?"

"Looks like they left one of their members behind as an assassin in case you happened to show up."

With each breath, she felt her strength and sense of identity return. "I saw the other three. They weren't in very good shape. Joe must have done considerable damage in the fight. The guy outside might have been hurt badly enough that the others would have considered him a liability." The words taxed her throat, but giving in to her physical limitation wasn't in her nature.

"Would he have had enough time to heal before we got here?"

"Apparently." Sere felt along the scar on her arm. Bart's blood was like vodka mixed into a Bloody Mary: only detectable as a lightheaded realization that things were about to get dangerous. "We need to help save Jennifer."

"How do you propose doing that? You're too weak to ride, let alone fight. I know you heal fast, but getting back to fighting strength is a different story. Do you even know where she is?"

Sere really wanted to get up and kick his ass, but unfortunately, he was right. *Fuck, Joe. Did you have to tell him about all of my vulnerabilities?* "They were in a johnboat headed back toward the swamp. Joe and Fisher were in pursuit, but they were on foot."

Bart stopped filling the steamer trunk and stared out toward the water. "They could be headed back this way. You said you and Jennifer couldn't be in the same place at the same time. How bad would it be if that did happen?"

"Best case, Jennifer ends up thinking she has a twin sister no one told her about. Worst case, we open the hellmouth for all the demons to escape."

Bart turned to her with wide eyes. "That would be bad."

"I'm joking. Even if Professor Yates didn't have security features in place regarding his projections, me meeting Jennifer wouldn't bring about the apocalypse."

"That's not funny."

Watching your reaction was, she thought. But she could see that from his perspective, all hell being set loose probably wouldn't be a laughing matter. "I'll try to be more understanding of your mortal sensitivities."

"Doesn't change the fact that our enemies are probably barreling down on us as we speak, and we're kind of on our own out here."

She ran over the list of potential allies and known foes. "Even if I could bribe the gator hunters to be on my side, they aren't going to risk the swamp after losing so many of their comrades. I can't trust your biker friends to be of much help, plus they're too far away. We don't have the time or transportation to call in Lefty's alligator navy. That pretty much just leaves Joe and whoever he was able to round up. He's like a bloodhound—he won't stop until he's found his prey—but the demons have a pretty big head start and maps of the swamp."

Bart turned back to the water as if he expected to see the

doppelgängers' boat far out on the horizon. "And you're in no condition to hunt for them even if we did have a way out there." He flexed his ass as if getting ready to sprint toward the end of the dock.

"I know what you're thinking," she said, "and the answer is no. I'm not letting you go out there alone. I know I said you were in charge of all things militarily tactical, but going out there without backup is just foolish, even for a Navy SEAL."

He nodded. "I know." He finally turned to her. "What kind of hairbrained scheme have you come up with?"

She rubbed the sides of her arms to increase her circulation. "We can't be positive this is where they're headed. Just because it makes sense to me doesn't mean the doppelgängers will follow my logic. They don't even know for certain this is where we are. You're really going to hate this a lot, but do you think you could give me a ride out to the closest of Joe's hidden caches?"

"Beats sitting around here on the sidelines, waiting to be attacked."

"You're really not going to tell me your plan?" Bart asked as he straddled his Ducati.

Sere climbed on the miniature back seat behind him, pressed her legs to his, and wrapped her arms around his blood-soaked leather jacket. "Just get me to the cache. Once we're safe, I'll lay it out, but you're not going to like it."

"Each time you say that, I reconsider blindly going along

with whatever you have in mind. I'm only taking you out there because I'm convinced the demons are coming for you, and Joe's is the logical place for them to start." He fired up the Monster and let the clutch out. The tire under Sere's ass spewed rocks into the trees with more violence than her shotgun.

As far as she was concerned, straddling her motorcycle and tearing off down the winding country roads was about the best experience life had to offer. Being at the mercy of another rider, however, was one of the worst. *At least Bart knows what he's doing.* She leaned forward and cuddled her cheek to the back of his broad shoulders in an attempt at making the best of the situation. Pressing her crotch against his muscular ass while straddling the intensely vibrating engine had its advantages.

Like the man himself, the bike required plenty of room to maneuver. Though it wasn't how she handled her more agile Triton, the way he took the corners in wide sweeping curves exhibited a gentle, understated command. She could easily envision falling asleep nestled in his strength.

He took a tight turn onto a dirt road and craned his head around to her. "Joe said the cache was off this unmarked road. He made me memorize the Google image. Any idea what we're looking for?"

She lifted her head off his back like a child waking up from a nap. She had to arch her body up along his to look over his shoulder at the road ahead. "Look for something abandoned. He's a big fan of old shipping containers, but don't get too hung up on size."

Bart took his hand off the handlebar and pointed toward

the far end of a lagoon. "Like an old half-submerged school bus?"

Sere had hoped for a less challenging approach. "Yeah, that would be something Joe would pick."

Bart pulled the Ducati behind a briar patch and shut down the engine. "Guess we're going to have to swim for it."

She hopped off the back of the bike, rejuvenated from the ride. "Wish I'd brought my saddlebags." She unbuckled her holster and bullet belt. *Get my clothes wet, or let Bart see me naked again?* She waited for his lead.

He stretched his legs and lifted his crotch from the metal gas tank. Having a passenger, even one as small as Sere, meant he'd been forced hard against the unyielding vibration. She bit her lip as she checked out how large the bulge in his pants had grown. *That has to hurt.*

As if oblivious to her stare, he pulled off his already-ruined leather jacket and tossed it onto the motorcycle seat. With one lascivious look into her eyes, he unzipped his leather pants. "I'm game if you are."

Fine. It's not like you haven't seen me naked before. She unfastened the front metal clasps of her leather bustier and exposed her small breasts to the warm night air—and to Bart's gaze. "I'm not doing a striptease for you. We have demons to kill." Even as she said that, she kind of hoped he'd take his time. *I've got a right to enjoy seeing him strip for the first time.*

He didn't even try being discreet as he stared at her. "If there's one thing I've learned, there's no point in denying life's little pleasures when they present themselves." He pulled the front of his skintight pants out beyond the bulge and yanked them to the ground. The powerhouse muscles of his legs put his arms to shame.

She found it hard to simultaneously breathe and control the saliva that filled her mouth. *Okay, that's one tight body. I can be forgiven for leering a little.* She was so mesmerized by his physique, and by the throbbing cock in his shorts, that she barely noticed her hands pulling off her tights. She waited to see how far he'd take the dangerous game. His removal of the pair of expensive leather riding pants was necessary, but dropping the black mesh briefs would be an act of pure vanity. *That thing looks downright disposable.*

He nearly tore the underwear down his legs. She stood stone-still, staring at his Adonis-like body. The doppelgängers she'd chosen for sexual exploits in hell had nothing on Rampart Thibodaux.

"Wow." The word just escaped her mouth as if she'd exhaled it.

"I'm glad you approve. Now, as you said, we've got demons to kill."

And you'd do a damn fine job of it with that shaft.

Feeling self-conscious about being the straggler, she shimmied her panties off and laid them over the rest of her clothing on the motorcycle seat. "Time to get to work. Joe likes rigging his caches with booby traps, so watch what you touch." To Sere's ears, every word that came out of her mouth sounded suggestive.

"Right." He turned and dove into the water like a fish who'd finally been released into his natural habitat.

God, what an ass, she thought as she hurried into the water behind him.

WITH THE DECORUM of the river to hide her nudity and lust, Sere swam after Bart to the waterlogged school bus. He arched his back—allowing her one last good look at his incredible butt—and dove toward the bottom. *You could at least wait for me to figure out Joe's traps.* Between her rapid breathing at seeing him naked for the first time and the physical exertion of the short swim, she was in no condition to go diving in after him. *Fucking injuries.*

The water settled to a perfect glassy calm where he'd submerged. In only the dim light of the moon, she couldn't see more than a foot below the surface. *You'd better not have gotten rolled by some alligator.* As one minute stretched to two, she took a couple of deep breaths to oxygenate her blood prior to searching for him.

Just as she was ready to jump up to make her dive, however, a moss-covered window of the bus fell open like a submarine hatch. "Come on. Joe has got quite the setup in here." Bart didn't even bother poking his head out the window.

She grabbed the base of the frame opening and heaved her body into the bus. Though half-submerged in the swamp, the interior was completely dry. Beyond the racks of knives, guns, and ammunition that she expected, a small two-person speedboat sat on rails, aimed at the rear doors.

Bart leaned into the craft to inspect the controls. "I'm guessing he has this set up for a quick escape."

She tried not to stare at his dangling cock while he stood

bent over. "Sounds right. Joe tries to plan for every contingency."

Why am I finding it so hard to say Joe's name while staring at Bart's naked body? Get it together, girl. You are not cock-hungry Jennifer.

Bart straightened up and faced her. His erection nodded ever so slightly as if saying, *Caught you looking.* "So I've got you out here. Time to fess up. What's this secret plan that I'm going to hate?"

She eyed the ever-present backpack stashed below the weapons, which contained her personal med kit. "Do you trust me?"

From his changing facial expressions, she could practically see him beat back the snarky response. "Not when it comes to your personal safety. You rush into dangerous situations like nothing can hurt you. You're no superhero."

But I am. "I need you to hook me up to the med kit. I'll tell you how to adjust the settings."

Bart's squinty eyes and tight lips let her know that Joe hadn't given him the abbreviated instruction manual to the paranormal first-aid kit. "Tell me you just plan to advise Jennifer on how to escape."

Damn you. With her secret ability to control Jennifer's body exposed, there wasn't much point in playing coy. "I'll only take over her body as a last resort. Help will be on the way, but I can't leave her out there on her own."

He ran his hand along his SEAL tattoo. "Sounds risky. At least I'll be here to monitor your progress."

Sere hoped he wouldn't be there. "How good are you at hacking technology?"

He broke eye contact and turned toward the wall of weapons. "I don't like talking about it."

She walked up and punched him in the shoulder as hard as she could. He barely flinched, though his cock and balls swung like bell clappers. "I'm standing naked in front of you and not for the first time. You've seen me hooked up to my real and slicing the head off a demon, and your answer when I ask you something personal is 'I don't like talking about it'? Too fucking bad, asshole. Spill. What do you know?"

"It's classified. What do you need me to do?"

That was just another bullshit answer, but if he could do what she asked, she didn't really need the details. "Your cousin said all of the boats on the swamp have GPS installed. Joe's little runabout over there is sure to have the latest in marine technology. Think you could hack into the system and find the demons?"

He tightened his lips into a fine line. "Normally, it wouldn't be much of a challenge, but around you, any wireless system loses signal."

She crossed her arms at her stomach and waited to see how long it would take for him to put two and two together.

"Wait a minute. You don't expect me to hook you up to Jennifer without the professor's fail-safes then *leave* you while I go tearing after the doppelgängers in Joe's boat? You're right. I hate that idea a lot."

She put her hand on his muscularly solid chest. "I'm not

going to get stuck in her. I promise. There's a clock built into the connecting program. Just make sure you give yourself enough time to reach her." She let her hand explore down to his navel. "Oh, and you might want to put some clothes on. Jennifer gets a little obsessed by men's bodies." *And she's not getting yours.*

"Just don't get cocky," he said. "That woman doesn't have your muscle memory."

"No kidding. It's been nearly a decade since she ran the cheerleading squad, and she's had a kid. You don't have to remind me."

Bart grabbed her hand but didn't remove it from his rock-hard abs. "Are you sure this is such a good idea?"

Bart, the constant worrier. How ever did you survive SEAL training?

"We can't expect her to make a break for it on her own," she said, "and waiting for Joe to show up is too risky. I trust you."

"Just don't do anything stupid. If everything goes according to plan, all you'll have to do is escape. Wait for me to confront the demons, then get out of whatever restraints they have on her. Once you're free, swim as far from their boat as you can. I'll grab your shotgun when I pick up my clothing. Those doppelgängers won't know what hit them."

JENNIFER HUDDLED, shaking, in the front of the boat, with her arms wrapped around her knees. Her hands and feet were tied with old twine that stank of chicken fat and dead alligator. With each turn of the boat or ripple on the river, spray hit her until she was drenched from head to toe. Her new silk blouse was ruined as was her cute black skirt.

"Why are you doing this to me?" she cried. But no matter how much she begged, the men who had abducted her kept on like robots.

Sere had been a mental passenger in Jennifer's life enough times to know when to keep quiet, but something about this union was different. She wasn't a part of the homemaker. Her emotions were still her own, and those consisted more of lust for the muscular, naked bartender than anger and fear at not being in control.

"You're going to be okay," Sere said inside Jennifer's mind.

You don't know that, Jennifer thought. *Where the hell were you when I ran from the house? I went out to the park, hoping to find the bravery and strength that saved my poor Bobby, but you weren't there. I was just the scared, useless little girl I've always been.*

Sere made her usual threat calculation, only this time, the field was purely mental and she wasn't facing an adversary. Jennifer could hear her if she talked, but Sere's thoughts didn't move her real's body. They were two distinct spirits this time. *Interesting. Must have been that idiotic blood transfusion. My body's now made from more than this woman's projection, so I can't just step into her skin.*

"I'm here now," Sere said. "I want you to calmly look around at the others in the boat. I need to see their weapons."

Like I would even know how to shoot a gun, Jennifer

responded, but she slowly turned her head as if filming with her husband's camcorder.

An arsenal of rifles, long-handled boat hooks, and knives were stashed in an open bait locker along the side of the boat behind two of the doppelgängers. They were expecting a fight. The third demon stood at the controls.

"Now, look over the side of the boat."

The view though Jennifer's eyes shook so violently from side to side that Sere didn't need to hear the objection. *This is going to be more of a challenge than I expected*, she thought.

"I know you're scared," Sere said. "You have every right to be, but you're stronger than you think. I'm going to talk you through this. All you have to do is follow my instructions."

Can't you do it for me? Jennifer asked plaintively.

I'm not taking possession of her. Sere's mental declaration was less an answer than a promise, but she had to keep it to herself. Jennifer didn't need the confirmation that there was another person inside her, or the woman really would go insane. "Help is on the way. The men who were chasing you weren't out to hurt you. They know you're in trouble. You just have to be brave."

When I saw the guy dressed all in black, I got so scared. I just ran.

"It doesn't matter now. But since he wasn't working with these men, you have to conclude that he was trying to help. He'll still be trying to rescue you." Sere chose her words carefully. Convincing the woman to believe her about who was trustworthy and who wasn't seemed like an impossible task.

What do you want me to do?

"That's my girl. Keep watching the men. When we get the opportunity, we're going to take one of those knives. Don't worry. I'll tell you what to do when the time is right."

Are you crazy? I don't know how to fight. She quivered so hard her teeth chattered.

"Listen to me. I've got one job, and that's to keep you safe. I'm not going to ask you to do anything I know you can't. So if I tell you to do something, it's because I know you can. I've seen you in action. Just trust yourself. You're not going to attack anyone, but when the fighting starts, you're going to need to get out of the way, and that means needing a knife to cut your bonds."

From behind Jennifer's eyes, Sere registered a trembling nod.

"Okay. I need you to watch and listen. When the rescue boats close in, things are going to get busy in a hurry. That's when you'll make your move. Look at the guy closest to you."

Jennifer looked down at the dude's heavy work boots. Whoever was behind all the demon invasions was getting smarter. Sending a CPA's doppelgänger really didn't make any sense. At least the guy in front of her looked like someone accustomed to the outdoors.

"That's good, Jennifer. See how he has the knife between his sock and shoe? There's no leather sheath. That means he doesn't know how to use it very well."

Like I do? Jennifer thought. *That guy must be two hundred pounds of pure muscle. He'd swat me like a bug if I tried to get that close.*

"If he's distracted, he might not notice. He's just one option. Now, look up his leg to his belt."

The scan was painfully slow. The demon wore torn blue jeans caked in mud. From the dark wet patches at the cleanly sliced upper leg, Sere could imagine the fight he'd had with Joe. *Slice hard, then jab. Try to disable your opponent at the legs, then move in for the kill.* The combat lesson was still fresh in her mind. At the strained leather belt, Jennifer's eyes stopped moving. A snub-nosed .38 pistol was stashed in the back of his pants.

"Okay, he's not our boy. Though he might not know how to use a knife, that gun is all I need to see to know we don't want to mess with that one. I need to see his torso."

Why? Jennifer protested. She clearly wanted no part in the evaluation, let alone any potential fight.

"I need to know how big a threat he is. Once the rescue team shows up, we can direct them on the guy in charge. Just look at his shirt. You don't want to make eye contact with him."

Jennifer shakily nodded. Like the pants, the sweat-stained cotton shirt was more befitting a worker than a foreman. The battle scars were as Sere had expected. A long horizontal cut that would have dropped a normal human still had glistening wet blood dripping all along it, but the scar on the demon's stomach was little more than a pink gash. *A soldier, not a commander, but one who knows what he's doing. That's probably why he's stationed close to Jennifer.*

"Very good. One down, two to go. Let's have a look at the goon in the middle of the boat."

Doppelgänger number two sat against the side of a

storage locker with his hands over the rifles like a human weapons closet. His cowboy boots were a little too clean and new. The black jeans could have been from a city boy trying to look tough or a country kid who'd just cashed his paycheck and wanted to look good for his girl. The silver chain at his waist, connected to a studded belt, confirmed Sere's impression of him as someone out of his depth. The gleaming black knife handle that projected up from the back of his belt didn't even have fingerprints on it.

"Look at his face."

Jennifer kept her head down but lifted her eyes to the young man's face as he stared out over the swamp. He was young and clean-shaven. The look in his eyes was that of an innocent trying to look tough. *He's our boy*, she thought, but confirming that to Jennifer would only make her stare at the kid until someone noticed.

"And last but not least, have a look at the dude behind the wheel. Take your time."

Her eyes moved down and across to the middle of the boat. Jennifer's eyes moved tentatively, focusing on the steering-console area until she got to the demon's hands. They were so coated in blood that the metal controls were dark red where he'd touched them. One look at the steel resolve in the pilot's face told Sere all she needed to know. This was the ringleader. Her pulse quickened.

Sere assessed the options. *His hands are busy driving the boat, and we're moving at approximately ten miles an hour through the swamp. One good backflip off the center thwart, and I could foot stomp that ugly mug backward into the river. Even if he did cut the throttle, our momentum would take us clear of the assgänger. Then it would only be a matter of grabbing the boat hook from the side opposite doppelgänger number two, and with one good swing, I'd have dispatched him as well.*

Sere mentally shook her head. She was in Jennifer's body, and unless she was willing to take possession, there was no way the woman could make the quick moves. *Stick to the plan*, she thought.

"You did very well, Jennifer. Now, try to relax. Help is on the way, and I'll be right here with you the entire time."

THOUGH SERE REMAINED on high alert, the eyes she depended on for information were half-closed again. "Wake up."

I don't want to. I've had a bad couple of days. I've done more running than I have in years, been abducted and dragged out to this smelly swamp, and I just want to go home. Why can't you let me sleep?

At least the woman was showing some backbone. "Up!" Sere insisted.

Jennifer worked back up to a sitting position with her hands around her legs and peered around in the dark. There were no lights, just trees looming out of the swamp like spectral spirits out to snag her soul. "Where are we?"

That was a remarkably good question. If they'd been headed toward Joe's cabin, they would be encountering signs of civilization along the shoreline. Sere analyzed the smells that wrinkled Jennifer's nose. *Rotting wood, animals, and fragrant night flowers. We're headed for the deep swamp.*

Sere went stone quiet to prevent Jennifer from getting even an emotional whiff of what she was thinking. They were headed for the hellmouth. The ramifications of taking a living person down to hell against her will were too numerous for Sere to consider. *Come on, boys,* she thought. *Move your tight military asses.*

As if obeying her command, the high-pitched whine of a speedboat pushed to its limit registered in the distance. Bart had never been one for subtlety.

"Time to get to work, Jennifer. Fold your knees under you as if you were about to be sick, and rest your hands on the deck."

I am about to be sick. The woman did as instructed. *Is that noise what we're waiting for?*

"Yes, and fortunately, your abductors are too focused on the route ahead to notice—so far. They'll figure it out at any moment, though. As soon as they do, the guy at the controls is going to hit the throttle. When the boat lurches, act like you lost your balance and lunge toward the guy in the middle of the boat. We need that knife he's got sheathed at his back."

Whether out of exhaustion, irritation, or resolve, Jennifer hunched down, ready for the attack. *Once I've got the knife and cut my bonds, what do I do?*

"One thing at a time. Your abductors are going to have their hands full fighting off the men that are headed this way. Stay low. We'll have to see what happens. Just do what I tell you."

I can do that.

Sere wasn't sure if Jennifer's words were a response to

her directions or a means of reinforcing the woman's resolve. As was always the case in battle, time took on the quality of a slow-motion film. She saw the man throw the throttle to full speed before yelling to his comrades. He'd given them no time to prepare themselves, and their disorientation worked in Jennifer's favor. The woman sprang her legs out straight like a frog leaping from a lily pad. Her head smacked right into demon number two's butt as he stared mindlessly out at the water. Fumbling like a virgin trying to get into a boy's pants for the first time, she grabbed for the knife with both hands. He might have noticed her if he hadn't fallen overboard.

"Now what?" Jennifer said out loud. In her state of panic, she'd forgotten that Sere wasn't actually standing next to her.

"Get down on your stomach so they can't see what you're doing, then cut the ties. Hold the knife with one hand and run the other back and forth so the zip tie cuts along the blade's edge." Sere was amazed she even had to explain this. Describing how to use a knife was like talking to a child.

The boat swung violently to the right, causing Jennifer to lose her balance and land in the pile of guns. *Really? You have to tempt me like this?* Sere thought. She struggled to resist the urge to take control of Jennifer's body and join the fight, like being an alcoholic holding a bottle of whiskey up to her mouth but keeping her lips closed.

Bullets whizzed over her head as Jennifer frantically sawed at the bonds. "Now what?" she kept repeating over and over as if asking what further travail she would encounter.

The boat cornered so hard that water flowed in over the gunwale. "This is your chance, Jennifer. Slip over the side."

Are you crazy? There are snakes and alligators in the swamp. I'd rather get shot than eaten.

"Damn it, woman, do what I tell you. Do it now before he straightens out the boat!"

But before Jennifer could whine a counterargument, something hit the side of the boat with such force that she rolled out into the river. The shock caused her to gulp in a mouthful of the putrid water. She tried to swim, but this wasn't the nice clear water of the pool at the gym. She figured out which way was up only to find herself staring at the bottom of a boat roaring over her head. *I'm going to die.*

"No, you're fucking not! Roll over and look at the bottom of the river."

Even without being directly connected to the woman's soul, Sere could tell that if Jennifer wasn't already drowning, she'd have sucked in another lungful of water. As far as the woman could see were overlapping two-inch-wide reptile scales.

Lefty! Good boy! Nice tail wag to dump the boat.

Sere hoped her enthusiasm would seep through into Jennifer's fears. "Grab hold. He's our friend. What do you have to lose?"

Jennifer reached down and grasped Lefty's massive shoulders. Like an underwater personal watercraft, the gigantic gator jetted away from the boats. When he surfaced, he nosedived into the riverbank, causing Jennifer to tumble over his head. She landed hard on her back, the impact driving the water from her lungs. She lay gasping on the sandbar while staring right into the open coffin-sized jaws of the monster.

Sere really wanted to reach out and pat him on the head. "Don't worry. That's his way of smiling. He's just happy you're okay."

"He's got a fucking terrifying way of showing it!" Jennifer screamed.

A loud blast echoed in from the swamp. "One demon down," she told Jennifer. "Only my four-barrel shotgun makes that much noise. Bart wouldn't waist those shells unless he was certain he had his prey in his sights."

"What the hell are you talking about?" Jennifer started crying again. "I'm really losing my mind this time, aren't I?"

Damn it. I knew better, Sere thought.

"You're fine, just in shock. Don't worry. This will all be over before you know it. Focus on Henry and Bobby. They're going to be so relieved to see you. Stay strong for them."

he bump that should have deposited Sere's soul back into her doppelgänger body yanked hard at her stomach but failed to break the connection. "It's time for me to go."

"No!" Jennifer screamed. "I won't let you. For the first time in my life, I've been brave. I'm not letting that go."

The technological pull continued to rip at Sere's soul, but Jennifer was holding on like a kid who'd just caught a Mardi Gras coconut from the Zulu King himself. *Do I tell her I'm not a part of her and see her lose her mind, or let her think bravery is some magical force that just shows up and leaves when it wants?*

Bart swung the small high-speed boat up to the shore. Fortunately, Jennifer refrained from making an outward statement about the half-naked muscular hero. But her wide unblinking eyes and watering mouth were enough for Sere to know the housewife would gladly agree to any sexually deviant idea that might pass through the Navy SEAL's head.

That man should be posing for the covers of romance novels. I'd read every one, Jennifer said.

"Don't give him any ideas. And don't get any yourself."

Bart jumped out of the boat like a navy commando, surveyed the area to make sure they were safe, then bent down next to Jennifer. "Can you stand?"

Jennifer's comical attempt at sitting up shouldn't have fooled anyone. "I don't think so," she told Bart.

"Bullshit," Sere said. "You are so fucking transparent."

You're right about the fucking part. Jennifer held her arms out limply, hoping to be picked up.

Bart's sinewy forearms closed in around her like boa constrictors. One hand snuck under the remains of her silk blouse and grasped her below the side of her breast.

Why did I wear a bra? Stupid. But then, no one told me I'd be saved by Adonis.

Bart's other hand grasped her far leg. With one clean jerk, he had her off the ground and held tight against his sweaty rock-hard chest.

Come here often, sailor? Jennifer peered into his heroic dark-brown eyes.

Sere was more than a little disgusted and fervently wished she could return to her own body. "At least you have the good sense not to make an actual pass at him. Let me inform you that you're married and have a son, in case your hormones have caused temporary amnesia."

Maybe I could use that as an excuse, Jennifer thought.

Bart stepped over the boat railing and set her in the passenger's chair. "I'll have you home in no time."

Do you have to?

Sere focused on only the necessary vocal muscles. "Bart."

He stood stone-still and stared into her eyes. "Sere? What the hell are you still doing in there? We had an agreement."

She focused all her attention on making each word count. "Won't let me leave."

"Damn it!" He gunned the engine and raced toward the other boat that was idling out in the swamp. Alligators that were finishing up their meal of freshly sliced doppelgänger dove for the river bottom.

Standing in the middle of the johnboat, Fisher raised Sere's single-barrel blaster. "What is it? Do we have more company?"

Joe at the controls swung the boat parallel to his fiberglass skiff and peered past Bart to Jennifer. "Is she okay?"

You two should know better than to ask Bart more than one question at a time, Sere thought.

Big, beautiful, heroic, and dumb. God, I love that man, Jennifer thought.

"Sere's still connected," Bart said. "Something must have gone wrong at the cache."

With more agility than Sere suspected, Fisher jumped into the boat. "I'll go with you. I know a little something about being possessed. I can keep her calm."

Joe took off first with Bart right behind him. *Smarts before speed,* Sere thought.

Fisher leaned down next to the chair. "How are you feeling, darlin'?"

Look, old man, could you please just move over a foot or two so I can admire that hunk of man meat at the controls? Out loud, Jennifer managed to control her lust. "I've been kidnapped, dragged through the swamp, shot at, and fallen overboard into a river full of alligators. I've had better nights."

Bart throttled back to avoid overtaking Joe and yelled over his shoulder to Fisher, "Sere's not the one holding on. It's Jennifer who needs to let go."

Fisher sat on the back engine housing and nodded. "It's like magically being given all the attributes you always wanted, isn't it? Bravery, strength, self-confidence, a conviction that life is yours for the taking—they're all now a part of you. Who wouldn't hold onto that with all they've got?"

Jennifer blinked as if it was physically painful to shift her gaze from Bart's half-naked body to the gentleman next to her. "How did you know?"

"I'm possessed by a similar affliction. Though in my case, I'd happily be rid of it. Here's what I can tell you: what you're experiencing is nothing more than your personal conviction. Believe you're brave, and you will be. Stick to your beliefs, and you will be strong. Accept that you've made it this far in life by charting your own path, and you'll lose the self-doubt that doesn't serve any purpose. You don't need any magical spell to give you what you already have."

"But why should I give up something that works?" Sere could feel Jennifer's grip on her soul intensify. She was like a child not willing to give up her doll. What she didn't realize was this one had teeth.

"Aren't you missing that luscious ass?" Sere softly asked, hoping Jennifer would think the idea was her own.

Jennifer twisted away from the old man while pretending the movement was due to muscle fatigue. Once she was no longer facing the back of the boat, Sere continued flexing the muscles already in action to complete the body's three-quarter turn. When Jennifer faced the water, Sere made her flex her leg and back muscles so hard that she fell over the side.

Above the river's surface, both motorboats cut their throttles. Joe was the first to close in on the splash. The instant he had the motor shut down, he dove in.

Panic froze Jennifer sufficiently for Sere to perform her emergency water procedure. The first step was to get out of the confining blouse and dress that floated around her like ghosts trying to drag her to the underworld. With the shoes kicked off, dress shimmied out of, and back buttons of the blouse yanked open, Sere kicked hard toward the surface.

As soon as her head broke out of the river, she locked eyes with Joe, who was treading water three feet away. "Fight me."

He gave a single nod and dove under her. Sere only had partial control of Jennifer's body, and those muscles hadn't seen so much action since her wedding night. Jennifer kicked at the hands grabbing her ankles, but without Sere's help, her fighting and evasion skills were no match for Joe's Special Forces training. Like an alligator performing his death roll, Joe had her under the surface and twirling in all directions.

As she flailed, trying to figure out which way was up, she exhaled the precious air and refilled her lungs with water.

Even in the dimly lit murky gray-green water, Sere saw the telltale red hue of her demonic side taking hold. With a double-fisted hammer blow to Joe's head, she broke free of his grasp.

The panic in Jennifer turned to horror. Instead of swimming for freedom, Sere straightened out Jennifer's body and shot at Joe like a torpedo. "I'll bash him in the gut, driving the wind out of him, then drag him to the bottom."

I fucking have to breathe! Jennifer's thoughts reminded Sere of her first training session with Joe so many years ago.

"No, you don't. Not for at least another minute," Sere said.

But the woman's body was again no match for Joe. He arched his back and landed his knee right into Jennifer's temple. As her momentum dissipated, he grabbed her by the hair.

Let me go! Jennifer pleaded.

"I'm not the one holding you," Sere said. "I'm not stealing your life, and you're not taking mine. Accept that you're a wife and mother and not some badass warrior. Let go of me, and you can return to those you love."

SERE CAME TO, gasping for air, on the floor of Joe's hidden cache.

"Easy. Just focus on your breathing. You're going to be

fine." Polly had her hand at Sere's back like someone who'd just performed the Heimlich maneuver.

"What happened?" Sere felt as if she'd been hit by the bus when it sank into the swamp and had been trapped under it ever since.

"You were a damn fool—that's what happened," Kendell yelled from her lookout position.

"Now dear," Myles said next to her, "we've all been reckless a time or two and usually under your guidance."

"He's got a point." Polly unwound the bandage from Sere's head. "But it wasn't entirely Sere's fault this time."

"Stop discussing my actions as if you had a say in any of it. I'm not running a democracy." Sere struggled to sit upright. "Tell me what happened to Jennifer out in the swamp. Is she okay?"

Polly repacked the med kit. "They're taking her to Joe's cabin to give her a once-over—physically and spiritually. She sucked down a lot of swamp water and is in shock, but Joe and Bart agree she'll survive. Bart also wanted you to know they got all three doppelgängers, and Lefty's alligator contingent disposed of the evidence. Once Jennifer is settled in with Joe and Fisher, Bart said he'd ride your motorcycle down here."

"One more apocalypse averted." Sere's head and body hurt, which wasn't typical even after a fight with Joe. She nodded at Polly's gear. "Got any demon-strength aspirin in that thing?"

Polly glanced at Myles and Kendell, who were still focused on the swamp. "Later. We need to talk about that blood transfusion," she whispered as if that were some sort of solution to Sere's headache.

Like I had a choice about that. Sere kept that thought to herself. Clearly, Polly didn't want the others to hear about the transfusion.

16

$\mathcal{E}$ven by Sere's standards, it had been a long couple of days fighting demons—not that anyone outside of a select few would ever know about the latest averted apocalypse. Even those who were aware of her actions weren't likely to give her credit. If the ungrateful Northshore dudes did find out about the destruction of the murderers, they'd find some way to make it sound as if they were the ones responsible for the heroic effort.

As for Kendell, Polly, and the New Orleans contingent, the week was just another battle in a war without end. Only Bart had expressed his approval, giving Sere a good pat on the butt for her efforts, but that felt more like one teammate congratulating another than something more intimate. Given the choice, she'd have rather patted his luscious ass than the other way around.

By the time she returned to the city persona that she was still crafting, the late-afternoon sun was beating down on the Quarter. She had every right to be hungry and tired even though food and sleep weren't life necessities she required. As she walked down Decatur Street, the smells of cheese, pepperoni, and olives wrapped around her nose, making her mouth water. Never before had she wanted to take a bite out of something so badly, with the possible exception of Bart's perfectly toned bottom.

She reached deep into the pocket of the bloodstained bustier and pulled out a twenty wrapped around a business card. *Damn, Kendell. I guess if the tip didn't land in the jar, you forgot all about it.* She turned the card over and read the hastily scrawled note. "I'd love to get lunch sometime and discuss the beautiful music we could make together." *Blech. No wonder you left the twenty in the costume pocket.*

She figured one person's rejection was another's pizza. "I suppose I deserve a little reward for stopping another demon horde."

Beneath the heavenly aroma of melted cheese over baked crust, the brightly lit pizzeria smelled of cleaning solvents. From the way her boots stuck to the tile floor, Sere wondered when the place had last changed the water bucket. Turntables under heat lamps kept the pizzas warm in their countertop displays.

"I'd like a pepperoni and olive."

The woman behind the counter looked up from her romance novel, glowering. She was probably in the middle of a particularly steamy chapter. "How many slices?"

Sere slid the twenty across the counter. "The whole pie."

"Fine." The cashier finally set the book down and grabbed a box. Then she slid the pizza off the tray and into the generic brown cardboard. The crust had all of the structural stability of a twelve-inch uncooked flounder.

Sere grabbed a slice before the woman had a chance to fold the top down. She curled it nearly in half lengthwise and took a bite. "This must be the absolute best pizza in the world." She took another bite and savored the burning-hot cheese as it scorched the roof of her mouth.

The young woman leaned across the counter. "Lady, I work here, but that doesn't mean I have to endure your sarcasm. We stay in business exclusively due to hungover partiers looking for something salty and greasy to get them right for another night."

Sere decided her hunger had to be a remnant of her connection to Jennifer. That poor woman probably hadn't eaten at all before her abduction. If she had, she'd have been yakking all over the boat. "Rough night," she said, playing along with the hungover act.

The cashier leaned back as if justified in her assessment. "We get that a lot."

With the knowledge that even a college student would likely turn up her nose at the pizza, Sere devoured the slice on her way out the door. She only made it a block before the oily cheese, processed meat, and soggy crust made her stomach gurgle like it was filled with swamp gas.

A familiar army-boot-covered foot projected from the corner doorway. She balanced the pizza box on one hand like a fancy Italian waiter. "Your order is ready, sir."

The homeless dude edged his back up along the doorframe into the seated position. "You're back, and with food." His eyes fixed on the cardboard box. "I'm glad to see you're none the worse for your adventure."

"Just wanted to return the lunch favor." She took her spot on the lower step and opened the box.

He peered over his nose at the pizza then looked her in the eyes. "I need to get you a list of proper restaurants."

"Like you've got any room to talk. What was that fish, anyway? Gulf crapper?"

He wiped his perpetually dirty hand on his equally disgusting jacket then reached in for a slice. "Free food is free food. You wouldn't happen to have any mustard, would ya?"

"On pizza? No. I didn't think to pick any up," she said sarcastically.

He shrugged and began devouring the slice. "To what do I owe the honor?"

"Can't a girl just want to share a meal with a friend?"

He looked at her with glazed eyes. "Nope. Not in your case. You treat people the way a kid would treat her dolls—pretending we're real but not actually believing it. We've been watching over you since Kendell told us of your existence. In all that time, I've never heard of you spending time with someone simply for the conversation."

I didn't have toys, only doppelgängers. "That's not true," she said. But she thought back over her interactions independent of killing demons. "I dance at the club every chance I get."

He nearly spit out a mouthful of pizza as he laughed. "Dancing isn't conversation."

"It is if it's done right," she countered seductively.

"Fine, but even then, we're talking of a lovely young woman teasing equally handsome suitors." He pointed at the two of them. "This pairing ain't natural."

She picked up a slice from the high side of the box that had drained some of its oil into a small pond of yuck. "I'm not allowed to pick my friends because I'm young and attractive?" She began to see the advantage of keeping Jennifer alive and sane until old age. Switching her appearance on the spot might change the homeless man's impression of her.

He shrugged. "I'm not complaining. Just saying people, especially women, don't usually hang out with the likes of me for no reason."

Me neither. "Have you considered that you might prefer to be alone? You have a habit of driving people away. I mean, you do have a place across the river where you can get a hot shower and clean clothes. Kendell made sure of that." Sere waved at his overall appearance. "This grunge thing you've got going on isn't exactly inviting to most people."

He tossed his half-eaten crust into the empty box. "Point taken. What's your excuse? Because I don't see you hanging out with a bunch of friends."

He was more right than she wanted to admit. "I'm working on it," she said. "Trusting others isn't something that comes naturally for me. I'm beginning to see that I've been pushing people away with my snarky rejoinders. Letting people in isn't easy."

~

BACK IN THE LOFT, Sere slept harder than she'd ever remembered sleeping. She woke up to the sun streaming in the dormer window and the sound of a street sweeper cleaning up the ravages of the night's revelry. Above her head, her snakes dozed on the rafter, shaking the ends of their rattles sounding like old men snoring. Her body ached as she pushed off of the sagging mattress. Blood, mud, and demon crud covered her body where her clothes had been. The bustier and tights emanated swamp smells from a corner of the loft.

"Guess I owe Kendell a new Halloween costume."

It took an hour in the shower to scrub every inch of her body back to pink skin. Then she stood naked in the closet, wondering what she was supposed to wear. Her riding leathers made sense if she intended on running, but without an adversary, the fight-or-flight instinct felt misplaced. She ran her hands over the various band outfits. The steampunk gear projected a fun in-your-face attitude that she appreciated, but for once, she didn't want to play the provocateur.

"It's not that I want to fit in, but there has to be something I can wear that will let me talk to people without making some unintended impression." She pulled a pair of low-rider jeans off a hanger. The waistband hugged her along the same line across her hips as her bullet belt. The bohemian tunic that hung next to the pants looked like a hippie throwback, but the loose fit didn't restrict her movements. She synched a wide leather belt around her waist to replace the feeling of being armed with her shotgun.

Before leaving the apartment, she pulled on her alligator boots. "No way I'm leaving my knife behind."

Without much else to do with her day, she headed into Fisher's offices. Though she could spend her nights drinking and working off her pent-up energy on the dance floor, aimlessly wandering the Quarter only made her anxious for her next demon encounter. Fisher had said he could put her to work. Hunting down deadbeats and tax evaders might be a welcome change from combating serial killers and demons.

Linda looked up from her typing. "I wondered if we'd see you today. He Who Does Not Make Appointments is waiting in your office."

Sere did her best to keep her heartbeat in check. *I suppose a little excitement at seeing the one who saved my life isn't a bad thing.* When she walked into her office, however, the new mountain of files on her desk quashed her enthusiasm. "What's all this?"

"What you asked for," Bart said. "These are the people who've died by mysterious causes over the last week."

She gulped. "That's a lot of files. The sheriff's department must have their hands full."

He lifted one off the top. A little green sticky note was stuck to the front. "My cousin went through all of them. He used green for suspected safe—as in, an alligator probably did the deed—yellow for completely unknown, and red for suspected demon."

How considerate of him. "Feel like saving me the work of separating them out?"

He tossed the police folder back with the others. "Twelve demon-on-human murders and four unknown."

Damn, that's a lot of incoming doppelgängers. "Our boys were busy."

He nodded at the green Post-It. "Not just the demons. There's twenty-seven alligator-on-human deaths as well. We're talking a full-on demon and gator slaughter up there. Every person who can handle a rifle or drive a boat is joining lynch mobs. If something isn't done soon, we'll have a modern-day peasant uprising north of the lake. With the doppelgängers already dispatched, events are either going to turn toward a witch hunt of the innocent, an alligator massacre, or both."

"Your biker friends and Riley's posse made it pretty clear I wasn't welcome up there." She pulled out the bottle of Jameson's she kept in the bottom drawer of her desk.

"A little early in the day, isn't it?"

"I don't usually sleep, so it's all the same to me." She poured a generous two fingers into the tumbler.

"What's with doppelgängers and alcohol, anyway? Seems like a bar is always the first stop they make after leaving the swamp."

"Can you blame them? Most of my brethren are based on city folk. Imagine someone from the Quarter finding himself in the middle of a swamp and having to make his way back to civilization. Anyone would be a little parched after that ordeal."

Bart shook his head. "I've seen people drink out of relief. The look on those guys' faces was anticipation, like they'd been on the wagon for too long."

She turned the glass with the magical amber liquid in her hand. "From personal experience, I can tell you that alcohol gives me a break from the interdimensional tug-of-war that never lets up."

"Sounds like doppelgänger bullshit to me." He picked up the bottle and stared at the liquid like someone studying a deadly strain of bacteria in an uncorked glass beaker. "After my time in combat, I found it hard to relate to normal people. I saw everyone I met as either an ally or an enemy, and women were easy conquests. I started drinking because I thought it'd lubricate my interpersonal relationships— make things easier, you know? I was looking to dull my instinct to dominate. Actually, the opposite happened."

Yet you drank with me. I wonder why. "Now that you know better," she said, "you drink to increase the distance?"

"Now I drink out of fear." The intense look in his eyes told her how difficult the sentence had been to speak out loud. "I'm a Navy SEAL. Physical danger doesn't faze me, but when I sense a closeness developing that I can't control, my flight instinct kicks in. Alcohol helps me combat it, but too much can turn me into an asshole. Unfortunately, I can't usually stop myself from overindulging."

She could see a similarity in how she used alcohol. Life had a way of enticing her into its grasp, and drinking gave her a dispassionate distance from humanity. "You managed to control your drinking around me."

"You're not like most women. There's a sense of equality in our relationship."

"So I'm the ally, whereas most women are the enemy?" she asked.

"Something like that. You do keep me on my toes, but not in a combative way. When you started leaning on me, I began to let my guard down—someone that I respect putting their trust in me has a way of doing that. A shot or two with you knocks down my inherently snarky coping mechanism, but the honor you inspire in me prevents me from taking my drinking any further."

Though his openness intrigued her, Sere feared another question down the path of their relationship would make him tip the bottle to his lips, and once they let down their guards, they could end up anywhere. There were still life-and-death questions to be answered, demons on the horizon, and a woman who might be struggling with her sanity. Whatever emotions were building between them would have to wait.

"Tell me what happened to Jennifer after I got pulled out of her."

He set the bottle down and kicked his shoes up on her desk as if grateful for the change of subject. "She kept talking about an alternate self. That boss of yours in the next office is quite the talker. Each time Jennifer proposed something that hit a little too close to the truth, he found a way to make it sound like the attribute was inside her all along. By the time we got her back to the stream that cut through the park, she was more or less her old self."

"Hopefully, she doesn't freak out on her husband. Keeping that woman out of the loony bin is going to be a constant aggravation."

"Speaking of constant aggravations, any thoughts on when I should pencil you in for another rescue?"

That was a good question. Apparently, the doppelgängers couldn't just go through the door when someone died. Or maybe Sere's nemesis was just taking his time planning his next move.

"We had about three months between Monty and the gang of seven."

Bart dropped his boots from her desk. "Just don't spent the whole time at the bottom of a bottle."

Take me with you. The fleeting thought had overtones of Jennifer, but Sere couldn't deny that the idea of leaving the city and spending some quality time with Bart had its appeal. But she had to stay in the New Orleans. The demons would still see her as a beacon for leaving the swamp, and she couldn't expect him to stay just for her.

Sere turned the glass while watching the alcohol creep up the side like a spirit trying to escape. She returned the tumbler to her desk and pushed it toward the bottle. "If I intend on further understanding what it means to be human, maybe it's time I also faced this life sober."

BOOK LIST

Technopia Series:
(writing as Greg Chase)
Creation
Evolution
Damnation
Salvation

The Malveaux Curse Mysteries :
(writing as G.A. Chase)
Dog Days of Voodoo
You, Me, and the Voodoo Queen
Oops! I Voodooed Again
Voodoo You Love
Voodoo You Think You Are
Look What You Made Me Voodoo
Love Me Like Voodoo

The Devil's Daughter:
(writing as G.A. Chase)
Hell in a Head Gasket
Hell Bent for Demons

<u>Other Stories</u>
Through the Lens

ABOUT THE AUTHOR

G.A. Chase is the pen name for Greg Chase. He is a science fiction and paranormal author living in New Orleans with his wife, fellow author Deanna Chase, and their two shih tzu dogs. On any given day you can find him behind his computer, people watching in the Quarter, or out in his studio creating stories in glass. His glass work can be found at www.chase-designs.com.

www.gregchaseauthor.com